To Kill a Queen

Away from the stresses and dangers of his job with Edinburgh City Police, Detective Inspector Jeremy Faro looks forward to a peaceful holiday in the beautiful Deeside region of the Royal Estate at Balmoral Castle. He plans nothing more strenuous than to celebrate his aunt's ninetieth birthday and enjoy a little fishing in the company of his stepson Dr Vincent Laurie, who has taken up a post at the local Prince Consort Hospital.

But Faro's reputation travels with him, and without any chance to relax, his skills are called on by none other than Queen Victoria, in residence at Balmoral Castle. While he is flattered that the Monarch should require his assistance, Faro is somewhat put out to discover from John Brown that he is to track down whoever has killed the Queen's two favourite spaniels. It is not long, however, before Faro has a killing of far greater magnitude to concentrate on: Scotland Yard have got wind of a plot to assassinate the Queen.

Time is not on Faro's side. The conspirators plan to strike within the next few days, before the Queen returns to London. Certain that the assassin is already responsible for two unsolved murders in the area, and with the Queen unaware of the incredible risk to her life, Faro embarks on a nightmarish hunt for a merciless double killer – a killer who will stop at nothing to commit the ultimate treason . . .

To Kill a Queen

Alanna Knight

**MACMILLAN
LONDON**

First published 1992 by
MACMILLAN LONDON LIMITED
Cavaye Place London SW10 9PG
and Basingstoke

Associated companies in Auckland, Budapest, Dublin, Gaborone, Harare, Hong Kong, Kampala, Kuala Lumpur, Lagos, Madras, Manzini, Melbourne, Mexico City, Nairobi, New York, Singapore, Sydney, Tokyo and Windhoek

ISBN 0–333–57098–7

A CIP catalogue record for this book is available from the British Library

Typeset by Macmillan Production Limited
Printed and bound by Billing and Sons Limited, Worcester

To my dear Aberdeen friends,
Anne and James Logan;

and the 'Culter Gang':
Sheila and Rodney Jones
Joan and Pierre de Kock
Gwen and Angus McLeod
Françoise and Donald Macdonald
Evelyn and John Steele
Joyce and Ron Wright

and many more!!

Chapter One

As the train steamed into Aberdeen station, the promising morning of glittering sunshine was under threat from a shroud of mist creeping in from the North Sea.

The foghorn's dismal note did nothing to dispel the persistent chill and was less than welcoming to the two men who emerged wraithlike from the smoke enveloping the platform.

Both were fair-haired and blue-eyed but there all likeness ended. The elder had a countenance curiously in keeping with the legends of Viking raiders in the north of Scotland. Tall leanness concealed considerable strength. A somewhat arrogant face defied the popular fashion for beards. High of cheekbone and nose, only a mouth full lipped and well shaped conceded to curves and hinted at a gentler disposition than first glance suggested.

As for his companion, a frivolity of blond curls sought to escape from the tall hat he clasped firmly against a shrilly unpleasant wind. It cut like a knife, moaning through the open roofs, making its presence felt day and night. With a countenance curiously innocent and vulnerable, this younger man could have passed for seventeen.

But the appearance of both men was deceptive. Closer acquaintance might have detected tight-drawn precision, an ability to make rapid and often life-saving decisions about the younger man's almost cherubic countenance. And in the elder, a certain steeliness about the eyes told a tale of authority, of power and hidden springs coiled taut and ready for instant action. Here was a man used to danger, a man who could be loyal friend, or deadly foe.

His name was Detective Inspector Jeremy Faro. His companion who constantly deplored the lack of evidence of a maturity more befitting his chosen profession was somewhat surprisingly, considering the still youthful appearance of the elder man, his stepson, Dr Vincent Beaumarcher Laurie. He had just been appointed as locum tenens to the resident doctor at The Prince Consort Cottage Hospital at Beagmill on the edge of the Balmoral Estate.

Carrying their light luggage, they walked smartly towards the far end of the station where, almost invisible behind a platform high in wooden boxes, the train for Ballater was being loaded. Both men pressed handkerchiefs to noses. Even the strong breezes were no armour against the pungent aroma around them.

'High in coffined kippers,' muttered Vince.

'Aye, with everything boxed but the smell,' Faro added and Vince looked at him enquiringly.

'Did you write that?'

Faro shrugged. 'No. Read it somewhere.'

'Fortunate that you aren't here on business, Stepfather. Any self-respecting Central Office bloodhound would be put off by the scent, his nose permanently put out of business, I shouldn't wonder. Ugh!' Vince added, as they hurried aboard the waiting train.

The kippers were a delicacy destined for the Royal breakfast table at Balmoral where Her Majesty was very partial to Aberdeen's famous export. In one of the estate cottages Faro and Vince would partake of less redolent fare, notably the traditional porridge provided by Aunt Isabel, or Bella as she was known, a grand old lady on the eve of her ninetieth birthday.

Faro's mother was never slow to remind him of family obligations and her original intention had been to travel down from Orkney for this important occasion, bringing

8

Rose and Emily to be reunited with their father on Deeside. She had shown great enterprise by reserving accommodation in one of Ballater's excellent hotels on the excuse that Aunt Bella's cottage was quite inadequate for a whole family which included two grown men. But as they prepared to set out disaster had struck. Mary Faro wrote that the two girls had gone down with chicken-pox.

Faro was bitterly disappointed. Chances to see Rose and Emily were rare and ninetieth birthdays were even rarer. He had no desire to add to his aunt's distress by the absence of her heart's darling. Himself. Her favourite nephew, treasured by her as the son she had never had.

Throughout the years Aunt Bella had been his constant refuge in times of stress, providing a retreat whenever he was convalescing from illness, or from injuries resulting from violent encounters with criminals. Faro had many but, as his enemies grumbled, he bore a charmed life.

As for his children, he bore enough guilt and suffered enough sleepness nights for his neglect, real or imagined, of his motherless daughters, whose rightful place, according to Mary Faro, was with their father in Edinburgh. Diplomatically he tried to justify himself in the face of her reproaches – without ever revealing the constant dangers of his life with Edinburgh City Police.

He was a marked man, frequently the target for incidents from which he had narrowly escaped death, making light to her of broken limbs and gunshot wounds. But criminals were no respecters of a policeman's family and he knew from past experience that the presence of two small girls could add a nightmare vulnerability to his daily life.

His thoughts were distracted by Vince reeling up the carriage window and settling back into his seat gratefully.

'I suppose all you have to do is enjoy yourself for a few days, Stepfather. How do you fancy a life without crime for a change?'

9

'Exceedingly well. Let's hope there is nothing more unlawful than whisky illicitly stilled and salmon illegally gaffed.'

Unbuttoning his greatcoat, Faro took the brim of his tall hat between two fingers and spun it adroitly on to the rack above.

'How do you do that?' asked Vince in admiration.

'Trick of the wrist, lad. Something my late uncle taught me long ago at Easter Balmoral. Quite deadly, I assure you, with the skean dhu. But I wasn't considered old enough then for sharp knives.'

'I must say I'm looking forward to seeing Great-aunt again,' Vince sighed. 'I fancy a comfortable pastoral hospital where the patients are few and the population healthy. And uncomplicated. For a change.'

A slight tremble in his voice, another, deeper sigh, told all too bitterly how his own happiness had been recently blighted.

Faro regarded him sharply. Vince was staring out of the window. His eyes, suddenly bleak, reminded Faro, in the unlikely event of his ever forgetting the tragic details, how the lad's appointment as factory doctor in Dundee had been marked by heartbreak and near breakdown.

The lad was still looking far from well, but putting his faith in youth's resilience, Faro was confident that Vince would soon find the new job much more agreeable. And he hoped he would also find a more enduring love.

Meanwhile he was convinced that the splendid Ballater air would do the lad a power of good, with Aunt Bella's cosseting close at hand as an excellent substitute for Mrs Brook, their admirable housekeeper.

He hoped Mrs Brook was enjoying her few days' holiday in Perth. Deliberately he pushed to the back of his mind the ominous shadow that now hung over 9 Sheridan Place. He shuddered from the turmoil that must ensue should Mrs Brook's invalid sister, recently bereaved, need her constant attention.

A widower in a large family house, at the mercy of

inefficient servants, he saw himself seeking board and lodgings nearer the Central Office.

Staring out of the window he gazed at the magnificence of an undulating landscape which suddenly replaced his gloomy thoughts with the excitement and pleasurable anticipation of long-lost boyhood. For if there was any place on earth he could call his spiritual home, then it was Deeside. In that sad childhood summer after his policeman father Magnus Faro was killed, he had found healing with his aunt, and with his uncle a passion for fishing, albeit of the net and jar variety.

Gradually, he began to relax as every mile distanced him from a battle of wits with the villains who lurked behind the noise and grime of Edinburgh's High Street and continually harassed the Central Office.

There Superintendent McIntosh tended to be absent-minded about his chief detective's right to have holidays.

Grumbling as always, he had stared moodily out of the window. 'A deuced inconvenient time, I might say, Faro. I'm away to a family wedding in Aberdeen.'

McIntosh's expression had then changed to one of suspicion. 'Easter Balmoral, did you say? Near Crathie, isn't it?' And snatching a paper off the pile on his desk, he added, 'I thought so. Came this morning. Woman murdered.'

Pausing for reaction and finding none forthcoming, he demanded, 'Wouldn't have anything to do with your sudden desire to go up there, would it?'

Assured that this was a holiday and family occasion only, McIntosh sighed. 'Ah, well, in that case, I suppose if you must.' His impatient gesture signalled that permission was given somewhat grudgingly and the interview at an end.

About to leave, Faro turned. 'This murder case . . . '

'Person or persons unknown. That's the verdict. But between you and me, the evidence points to a jealous lover,' said McIntosh. 'Nothing you need concern yourself about.'

11

'Where exactly did it happen?'

'I was just reading it when you came in.'

But as Faro stretched out his hand towards the papers, McIntosh quickly covered them.

'Never you mind, Faro. You are on leave, remember.'

'I know that but—'

'But nothing. Case is closed and you stay out of it, Faro. We want no meddling, if you please. It's out of our province and the Aberdeen police won't thank us for poking our noses in. You know the rules,' he added sternly. 'Inspector Purdie from Scotland Yard is up there right now. Called in because of the proximity of Balmoral Castle, I imagine.'

When Faro mentioned this to Vince, the latter had smiled. 'Doesn't sound as if that one would be difficult to solve even for the local constable. The old crime passionnel again.'

'But presumably without enough evidence to hang him.'

'It happens.'

As stations flashed by and the Dee Valley unfolded its backdrop of grandeur, the two men were soon absorbed in the passing scene: gurgling streams, a gleaming ribbon of silvered river, and through lofty treetops a tantalising glimpse of turreted castle. Houses great and humble were overshadowed by the Grampian Mountains and Lord Byron's 'dark Lochnagar', its secret crevasses, even in summer, white-scarred with snow.

And everywhere towered the Scots pine, sole survivor of the most ancient woodland in Britain, the Caledonian forest, from which the bowmen of Flodden had taken their arrows and more than a thousand years before them, the Roman army had built their war chariots.

A pastoral scene, no doubt, but behind grey castle walls ancient when Mary Queen of Scots had visited the area, murder had been done. The bloodied pages of history opened everywhere. Here Montrose camped

12

with his troops on the way to the sack of Aberdeen. There Jacobites rode out for Prince Charles and a cause already lost, to die savagely on the battlefield at Culloden.

Now it seemed the butchery was limited to sport. As the Ballater train steamed into intermediate stations, carriages bearing coats of arms of noble houses awaited descending passengers. This was the heart of the shooting season. A few weeks and it would be over. Golden October would cover the land, the guns would be silent and deer, freed from man's ritual slaughter, would again go about the business of survival.

These sombre hills would echo by moonlight to that most eerie and primeval of sounds, the crash of antlers, the bellowing roar as King Stag went into the rut, a fight to the death to maintain his territory and his harem against the young bucks who annually threatened his supremacy.

When Faro spoke his thoughts, Vince's dry response was 'Sounds remarkably as if your old monarch of forest and mountain gave lessons to humans. Seeing that the deer were probably here first.'

There was no answering smile from his stepfather, suddenly aware of a more vulnerable monarch and the periodic attempts on the Queen's life. The fact that there were fewer at Balmoral, where she was considerably more exposed, never failed to surprise him.

Earlier that year in London a youth named Arthur O'Connor had pointed an unloaded pistol at the Queen, the idea being to scare her into releasing Fenian prisoners. Prince Arthur had made a weak attempt to jump over the carriage and save his mother. But John Brown was quicker; he seized the 'assassin', and was rewarded by his grateful sovereign with a gold medal, public thanks and an annuity of £25.

The Prince of Wales, who did not like Brown and enjoyed any chance of discrediting his mother's Highlander among his siblings, complained that his brother had behaved with equal gallantry and had been rewarded with only a gold pin.

As for O'Connor, the Queen greeted his one-year imprisonment with dismay and told Gladstone to have him transported, not out of severity but to prevent him trying again when he came out of prison. O'Connor received this verdict magnanimously, his only stipulation being that his exile should be in a healthy and agreeable climate.

The attempts reported in the newspapers had now reached six. It was a sombre fact, as Faro knew, that there had been many more. Never admitted to the popular press, such outrages were confined to the secret files of Scotland Yard and Edinburgh's Central Office, where Her Majesty's visits were Faro's responsibility and a constant source of anxiety.

'She is either the most foolhardy or the most courageous woman we have ever encountered,' he had told Vince.

'Puts her faith in the divine right of kings as sufficient protection, does she?'

'Possibly.'

'There is another explanation.'

'Indeed? And that is?'

'I'd hazard a complete lack of imagination,' was the short reply.

Faro shuddered as he now thought of that distinctive imposing figure, a boon to the caricaturists and eminently recognisable even at a distance. Stoutly clad in black dress with white streamered widow's cap, the Queen presented a perfect target for a desperate man with a gun.

And here she was at her 'dear Paradise' oblivious of danger. Most days found her traipsing happily about the lonely Deeside hills regardless of weather, without the small army that any cautious monarch would consider necessary. Her security guards, Captains Tweedie and Dumleigh, were sternly commanded to remain behind

14

at the Castle where they idled away many boring hours with nothing better to exert their wits on than playing cards as Her Gracious Majesty set forth accompanied only by her two favourite ghillies, Grant and John Brown. A formidable pair doubtless on their own terms, but no match for a determined assassin.

The Queen's only real protection, Faro knew from his aunt, was that in the country every newcomer was scrutinised and gossiped about via a bush telegraph system in many ways swifter and more efficient than the electrically operated version in Ballater. It was the simple truth that strangers could not walk these country paths without being observed, their presence questioned, remarked upon and neighbours alerted.

'Safe as houses she is,' Aunt Bella had said on his last visit. 'Ye ken there's not a blade o' grass stirs, not a new tree grows that isna' observed.'

When he had smiled at this exaggeration, she went on, 'Look out o' yon window. Naething but space ye'd guess? Aye, a body would ken that the whole world is empty. But it's no', that's no' the case at all.'

And sweeping her arm dramatically in the direction of the hills, she said, 'Fair seething wi' watchful eyes, it is. There's naught else for a body to do but mind ither folk's business. That's what.'

Upon that and upon the devotion and loyalty of her Scottish subjects and servants, the slender thread of the Queen's life and limb and the future of Great Britain and its colonies depended.

'Here we are at last, Stepfather,' Vince interrupted Faro's reverie and he saw that the vista of hills had been transformed into a town by a cluster of grey roofs and tall spires.

As they emerged from the station there were few remaining passengers unclaimed by the waiting coachmen. Faro was suddenly aware that he and Vince earned some curious glances, lending a comforting verisimilitude to his aunt's remarks.

15

At the station entrance a man saluted, came forward. 'Ye'll be for Mistress MacVae's place.'

'Indeed yes,' said Faro in surprise as the man took their bags and put them in the cart.

As they drove off, Faro glanced back over his shoulder. Among the faculties of self-protection developed through years of battle with violent men was a sixth sense warning him when he was under careful scrutiny, and he knew that he was being watched.

Now one solitary passenger remained. A heavily veiled woman was cautiously emerging from the station.

At the sight of him, her footsteps had faltered. And as he looked back for a moment he was certain that he knew her although her face was well hidden.

He laughed. What an absurd idea. He had obviously embarrassed the poor woman by staring so rudely. And her in mourning too. Gravely, politely, he raised his hat in her direction. There was no acknowledgement although her swift movement of turning her back suggested a guilty anxiety not to be recognised.

Faro glanced quickly at Vince but saw that the lad's attention was distracted by the handsome houses and shops as the cart trotted its way through Ballater's main thoroughfare.

Faro sighed, for a moment obsessed by memories as Vince's words regarding his own late unhappy love came back to him.

'I see her everywhere, Stepfather. I have to restrain myself from accosting innocent young women because they remind me, in a walk, or a smile, of her.'

Faro straightened his shoulders, suppressing a shudder of distaste. He must take warning from Vince's experience, since his own infatuation was now an inexcusably long time ago.

Vince was smiling at him. 'Well, we're on our way.'

'We are indeed,' Faro replied, casting aside his sombre thoughts.

And so the two men set forth, one intent upon dreams

16

of one day being Queen's physician and the other with dreams of a peaceful few days doing nothing more strenuous than a bit of fishing.

For Faro, however, a relaxing holiday on Deeside had in store a dreadful alternative.

Chapter Two

Their road led them past Knock Castle, a grim fortress staring down through the trees. Ruined and ancient, rooks flew forlornly around its desolate walls. A sad unhappy place, deserted, as if still haunted by the blood feud in which the eight sons of Gordon of Knock were extinguished in one day by their Forbes rivals.

Then a mile away from their destination at Easter Balmoral, through dappled trees, they glimpsed Abergeldie Castle. Rose-red walls enfolded a history of Jacobites in its dungeons and the spectral presence of French Kate burnt as a witch. But no ghosts tormented its present owner, the Prince of Wales, or the guests who attended his lively shooting parties.

Beyond the castle someone with an inventive turn of imagination had come up with an ingenious device of aerial transport. A strong cable stretched across the river. On it was a cradle in which two people were propelling themselves laboriously across to the opposite bank at Crathie, thus saving the walk round by the bridge which gave access to the main Deeside highway. Their efforts were being enthusiastically applauded by a band of shrill young people.

'Shouldn't fancy that myself,' said Vince.

Faro agreed. And as they travelled close to the river bank, he observed that Edinburgh's recent drought had also affected Deeside and the waters, normally noisy and frequently in spate, had their boiling foam tamed to a sluggish stream.

Even with hopes of fishing diminishing, Faro sighed pleasurably. Each visit to Ballater impressed him with the growing affluence he found there. Once the rich had come to the famed watering place at nearby Pannanich Wells, but the building of a railway and the added attraction of the Queen at Balmoral Castle had extended prosperity to Ballater. And the railway shareholders, aware of this growth in potential, had begged Her Majesty to allow the line to be extended as far as Braemar.

She would have none of it, however, unwilling to let her shy retreat be invaded any further, preferring to keep at some distance those holiday-makers from home and abroad anxious to follow the fashion set by the Queen of Great Britain.

As Faro silently approved her resolve, their driver drew aside and doffed his cap respectfully, giving way to an open carriage approaching rapidly down the narrow road.

'The Queen, gentlemen,' he muttered.

Faro and Vince just had time hastily to remove their hats as Her Majesty swept by, her widow's streamers dancing gleefully in the breeze. A pretty young girl with downcast eyes sat at her side. Princess Beatrice, Faro guessed, who looked as doleful and unhappy as the two ladies-in-waiting, their complexions somewhat blue with cold.

Standing on the carriage box, an imposing figure in Highland dress, rosy in countenance and obviously impervious to weather, was one of her Balmoral ghillies.

Chin tilted, the Queen moved a graceful hand and permitted herself a gentle smile in acknowledgement of the other vehicle.

'I'm certain she recognised you, Stepfather,' said Vince.

Faro felt that was extremely likely, for they had shared several encounters while he was in charge of her security in Edinburgh.

He smiled after the retreating carriage. The population

thought of their Queen as stern and unbending but Faro had noticed an almost coquettish tendency in her dealings with men, particularly if they were young and handsome.

This behaviour had not escaped attention – in particular her reactions to Inspector Faro who fulfilled all the conditions implied by the word attractive. In addition to towering over her physically, he could also make her laugh.

He was always taken by surprise by that hearty guffaw. It was startling in its almost masculine intensity and considerably more whole-hearted than the genteel merriment, if any at all, one might have expected to issue from the rather formidable Royal visage.

Remembering that laugh gave Faro cause to ponder as to whether there might be something after all in the press lampoons.

Vince asked, 'Would that be John Brown with her?'

'It would,' replied Faro. Could there be a grain of truth to justify the sneering epithet 'Mrs Brown'?

Memories as always came flooding back as the carriage climbed the steep hill to Easter Balmoral. In common with the Queen, Bella had been a widow for more than ten years. Her husband Ben had been ghillie at Balmoral in its humbler days before the present castle was built, when it was home to Sir Robert Gordon, who sold it to the enthusiastic Royal couple, the then young Queen and her adored Prince Consort.

Good Prince Albert had not lived long to enjoy his new home but the Queen still preferred her Highland retreat, the 'dear Paradise' she and Albert had created, to Buckingham Palace. Because of this rumours were rife that Her Majesty was in danger of becoming a recluse and a hermit. This did not pass unobserved in London. The gossip distressed and annoyed Mr Gladstone and the elder statesmen, in addition to presenting a ready target for the anti-monarchy faction.

The carriage turned a corner and there, nestling against

the gentle foothills of Craig nam Ban, sat the familiar cottage. Smoke issued from its solitary chimney, wafting the haunting smell of peat towards them.

But the breeze also carried a more acrid odour. Twenty yards distant was a burnt-out ruin. The two men turned, stared back at it.

'That was Nessie Brodie's cottage,' said Faro.

Vince sniffed the air. 'Must have been quite a blaze.'

'And recent. I hope no one was hurt.'

The road was rocky and uneven and the driver failed to hear his question. Doubtless Aunt Bella would regale them in some detail. But as they stepped down, the door flew open and down the path to greet them came Tibbie, whom Bella had adopted when she was a little lame girl many years ago.

There was no welcoming smile as she ushered them indoors.

'Yer auntie's no' here, Jeremy. She's in the hospital.'

And before Faro could do more than utter a shocked exclamation of concern, Tibbie went on, 'She's no' ill. Naething like that. She had an accident. Naething broken, thank the Lord, a few scrapes and burns. Did ye no' get ma' letter?' Faro shook his head. 'I posted it myself twa-three days sine. When Dr Elgin told her it wasna' likely she'd be fit to be home for her birthday. She was that upset. Said I was to write to ye straight away. I dinna ken why ye havna' got it.'

Her rising indignation refused to take into account that most letters from Aberdeen to Edinburgh, let alone Deeside, took at least a week to arrive at their destination.

Vince and Faro exchanged glances. How exceedingly fortunate that Mary Faro had insisted that her visit with the children remain a surprise, otherwise the disappointment would have been doubly hard to bear.

As Faro sat down at the kitchen table, the atmosphere overwhelmed him. He was ten years old again and nothing had changed. Walls steeped in a hundred years of peat

21

smoke, sheep's wool for weaving, the daily baking of bread and bannocks, all combined to open a Pandora's box of memories, happy and sad.

'What happened to Auntie?' he asked Tibbie. 'Was she on steps cleaning out the cupboards again?'

'No, indeed she wasna'. Worse this time. She went plunging into Nessie's cottage. Ye'll have seen it as ye came by. Or what's left of it. Bella saw the fire from the window here and awa' she went, fast as her legs would carry her, to rescue poor Nessie.'

'I presume she succeeded.'

'Aye, she did that,' said Tibbie proudly.

'At ninety,' said Vince in shocked tones, 'she should have known better.'

Tibbie turned a bitter look on him. 'She doesna' think she's ninety, ma laddie. She's that spry onyways, it's hard to credit. Why, I mind well—'

'Just tell us what happened,' Faro asked with desperate patience.

'She got Nessie out but a beam fell, mostly missed her, the Lord be thanked. Flying sparks gave her one or two burns and she got a few bruises. Nothing serious, as I've told ye, but her breathing was bad.'

'Shock, of course,' said Vince firmly.

'Aye, like enough. Onyways, the doctor thought she was better in the hospital considering her age and the like . . . '

'And Nessie?'

'Och, she's in the hospital. There's the pair of them in beds next to each other. Nessie's getting on fine. Nothing more than a dunt on her puir head. But she has a bad heart, ye ken. Bella's fair desperate to be home for her birthday. But there's no telling whether they'll let her out in time.'

She looked at them sadly. 'I doubt ye've come all this way for nothing though. If only ye'd got ma letter—'

'Not at all. We would have come anyway,' said Faro hastily. 'Vince has business here.'

22

'Business? What like business?'

'I'm going to work at the hospital. Help Dr Elgin.'

Tibbie greeted this news with delight. 'She'll be right glad to see the both of ye. She's that proud of Vince here. Always telling everybody what brains ye've got. And as for ye, Jeremy Faro,' she added turning to him. 'Ye were aye her favourite.'

And nodding vigorously, 'Aye, it's providence ye came. For she needs a wee bittie cheering. The nurses are having a hard time of it, I hear, she's that energetic. Having to keep to her bed is a sore trial.'

As Tibbie bustled about setting the table with remarkable speed for one so lame, she carried on a breathless non-stop monologue, one that neither Faro nor Vince had any possibility of turning into the remotest semblance of a conversation.

'—and what sort of a journey had ye? What like in Edinburgh?' Before Faro could do more than open his mouth to reply she had shot off again, answering the question for him.

By the time soup and bannocks appeared on the table, Tibbie was forced by the necessity of feeding her guests to let a few words pass their lips. Her occasional comments on their journey allowed their narrative to reach as far as Ballater.

'And we met the Queen on the low road,' Vince interposed smartly, thereby receiving an admiring look from his stepfather.

'The Queen, was it? Well, well.'

When he mentioned Princess Beatrice, Tibbie sighed. 'Bless her dear heart, she's that shy although she's past seventeen. Never has a word to say for herself when she comes visiting with her ma. The Queen still calls her Baby. I hear tell she doesna' want her to get married. Wants to keep her at home for company.'

'There was a ghillie with them, tall fellow with reddish hair and a beard?'

'That would be Johnnie Brown.'

23

Tibbie's attention was momentarily diverted by the need to remove bannocks from the oven and Faro, consoled that his aunt was in no danger, asked, 'What about this murder, Tibbie?'

'Och, I was just coming to that. Ye should have been here, Jeremy. Morag Brodie, niece to puir Nessie. Or so she claimed. Stabbed, she was—'

A sound from outside and Tibbie turned towards the window.

'There's Johnnie Brown now. The verra man himself,' she said excitedly. 'Goodness gracious, he's coming here.' Darting a fleeting glance in the one mirror to see that her mutch was tidy, straightening her apron and staring wide-eyed from Faro to Vince and back again, she prepared to open the door.

'What on earth can he be wanting? The Queen was in for her visit and a cup of tea just before the accident.'

The visitor who entered seemed to fill the whole room. Brown was a splendid figure of a man, in the Highland dress of kilt and sporran-purse (bearing the head of some fierce beady-eyed animal), with great strong legs in hose and brogans, and a plaid thrown carelessly across his shoulder to serve as robe or bed, where necessity arose. Perched on his red-gold hair was a Balmoral bonnet.

Gazing from John Brown to his stepfather, Vince decided that even in a much larger gathering, these two men could easily overshadow everyone else by their presence.

He recognised not only a physical similarity but felt as if the giants of old had materialised as they solemnly shook hands and took stock of each other. Both men, he guessed, had in common that rare quality of being shrewd observers of character. Perhaps both knew or had been brought up to the old adage, 'Look well on the face of thy friend, and thine enemy, at first meeting, for that is the last time thou shalt see him as he really is.'

Vince was surprised to see that Brown had been

24

followed into the room by a young man of his own age. Black-haired and blue-eyed, he would have been handsome but for the look of disquiet on his features.

'No, not disquiet,' Faro was to remark later, for it was a look he recognised. 'He reminded me of a sullen guilty schoolboy, grown-up but defiant still. And afraid.'

Introduced as Lachlan Brown, as they shook hands, Faro presumed the lad was kin to the newcomer. Was he John Brown's son, despite there being little resemblance between them?

Perhaps aware of their thoughts, Brown explained. 'Ma ghillie. Ye're no needed here, lad,' he added.

And Lachlan Brown, thought Faro, was very relieved indeed to take his departure. Throughout the visit as Brown accepted a dram from Tibbie and answered her bombardment of questions, Faro found himself intrigued by the identity of that oddly unhappy and watchful young man.

He had encountered many like him in his long career: those who, guilty or innocent, are made extremely uncomfortable and often rendered inarticulate by the presence of the law.

Why was Lachlan like that, Faro wondered? Certain that they had not met before, Faro felt there was nevertheless a haunting familiarity in Lachlan's appearance, an attitude, a gesture he seemed to recognise from a long way off. As if he was watching someone he knew well, distorted by a fairground's 'house of mirrors'.

Disturbed by the futile attempt to remember, he turned again to John Brown. Meanwhile his own lack of attention had been noted by his stepson who was busily comparing the two men.

Studying Faro critically, Vince again noticed his lack of sartorial elegance. The detective had deplorably little interest in clothes; they were to him at best a necessary covering rather than a prideful luxury.

Vince knew from his duties among the Edinburgh poor,

25

that all they could afford or ever hope to possess was one set of clothes, and that probably fourth- or fifth-hand. But why Faro should wish to emulate such unfortunates was beyond him. In a vain bid to fit his stepfather into the manner of life his position in society demanded, Vince had taken it upon himself to offer advice, which was accepted with good-humoured resignation and a complete lack of application.

Take the matter of boots. Faro failed to recognise that in his profession, which entailed an extraordinary amount of walking, a second pair was almost a necessity of survival. But Faro loved his old boots; the older they were the more he loved them, and the less willing was he to part with them.

Suddenly Vince realised why Faro had remained standing, partly hidden by the table. He was in his stocking feet. The new boots which Vince, ashamed of him, had insisted he 'break in' for the Deeside holiday had been removed and thrust aside, aching toes and a blistered heel thus relieved.

Vince now watched with interest and amusement what must happen next. Faro could not with politeness remain standing while John Brown was about to accept a seat and the refreshing of his dram. He must step forward and reveal all.

But even parted from his boots which lay accusingly distant, Faro was in command of the situation.

'You must excuse me.' He pointed. 'New boots, you know. Confoundedly painful.'

John Brown laughed, held up a hand. 'Man, think nothing of it. I ken fine the feeling. See these auld brogues o' mine. Ten year, I've had them. I love them like a lassie,' he chuckled. 'Man, the agonies I suffered breaking in yon new pair I must wear in Her Majesty's presence chamber and in her blasted drawing-room. Wummin, wi' their dainty feet and their dainty ways, they canna ken what we men suffer.' With a loud guffaw he slapped his bare leg delightedly.

26

And that was that. Suddenly, all embarrassment gone, both men were grinning at each other like apes, thought Vince.

Chortling happily, touching dram glasses, bound by common recollections, vying with each other on the matter of uncomfortable and abominable footwear, they stretched out their feet to the blaze.

Vince felt his presence was superfluous although John Brown tried politely to draw him into the conversation, putting him at his ease by talking softly and carefully, as if yon puir young Edinburgh laddie didna' understand the Highland speech.

Faro listened with some amusement, realising that they had the advantage since the Gaelic and not Lowland Scots was John Brown's native language.

As for Vince, he merely sighed. This was an all-too-familiar sore point, recalling the manner in which his Dundee patients treated him: as if he was still a wee school laddie and unaware of the ways of the world. If only they knew.

The next moment, Brown seemed to remember the reason for his visit. All jollity was suddenly wiped from his countenance, and he slammed down the empty glass on the table, refusing a refill.

'Inspector Faro, Dr Laurie,' he said, 'ye are doubtless wondering what has brought me to your doorstep with all haste the minute ye've arrived.' Pausing dramatically he looked from one to the other. 'Gentlemen, I am here on the Queen's business.'

Finding himself included, Vince sprang to the immediate and happy conclusion that there was in the offing an invitation to lunch or dine at the Castle. For Her Majesty's benevolence to the tenantry was well known. She was ever eager to dispense good works of a religious nature and for those unable to read, flannel petticoats and plentiful practical advice on child-rearing, a subject on which she was undeniably an authority. The statesmen and aristocrats of her realm would have been shocked

27

to be present and to hear their monarch addressed thus informally:

'Sit yeself down, Queen Victoria,' or 'Ye'll tak one o' ma' bannocks and a wee bittee crowdie cheese, Mistress Queen.'

In humble thatched cottages, the Royal gifts were received with no more awe or reverence than had the Queen been fulfilling the rôle in which she liked to cast herself, as laird of Balmoral.

While Vince and Faro waited for Brown to continue, Tibbie was hovering by the table, listening intently. She was the first to break the silence.

'And how is your mistress the day, Johnnie? She was verra gracious just afore the accident. We had a wee visit, ye ken, and Mistress Bella gave her a jar o' pickles to take back home to the Castle wi' her. She had admired them that much.' And with a shake of the head, 'The Queen will be that upset to ken Mistress Bella's in the hospital the now.'

'A sad business, Tibbie. But she's on the mend—'

'Aye, she is that, but—'

Faro listened helplessly. His curiosity about Brown's visit thoroughly aroused, he longed to get to the point. But unable to stem the tide of conversation by which Tibbie had diverted her visitor's attention he occupied himself with some minor observations.

The timing of Brown's visit suggested urgency since after setting down his Royal mistress at the Castle he must have picked up the lad Lachlan and set off immediately for Easter Balmoral.

The inescapable conclusion was that 'the Queen's business' was vitally important. Faro also suspected – if their earlier encounters were anything to go by – that it was likely to prove both uncomfortable and unpleasant.

He was right. Brown finally managed to extract himself from Tibbie's well-meaning chatter by standing up abruptly and snatching his bonnet from the table.

'I have words for your ears, Inspector. Perhaps you'd be good enough to step outside a minute.'

Thrusting feet hastily into boots, Faro followed Brown into the tiny garden. Before Brown carefully closed the door behind them, Faro had a glimpse of Vince's startled and rather crestfallen expression as Tibbie declared:

'Good gracious, lad. I hope everything's all right up at the Castle and that no one's been pilfering the silver—'

Brown heard it too. At Faro's enquiring glance he shook his head. 'More serious than that, Inspector. Much more serious.'

Was Brown about to discuss the Crathie murder? Or was the Queen in danger?

As he thought rapidly about how he could deal with such an emergency single-handed, Brown continued. 'Aye, this matter concerns the Queen's twa wee dogs.'

'Dogs, Mr Brown, did you say?'

'Aye, man. Dogs. Twa o' them wandered off and were found dead, still wearing their collars. Shot.'

Brown paused, regarded Faro intently. 'The Queen's verra upset. Verra. I'm at my wit's end, Inspector. Made all the usual enquiries but we canna' find their killer. The Queen will be verra severe on him. Royal property and the like, *lèse-majesté* and so forth.' With a shake of his head, he added, 'I wouldna' be at all surprised if it was the jail for him when we get him. And that, Inspector, is where you come in.'

'Me?' Faro's voice quavered a little.

'Aye, you, man. Who else? When the Queen saw you on the road back yonder she says to me: "There, Brown, there is your answer. Inspector Faro. How very fortunate that he is here. He will know exactly what to do. He is a policeman, after all. He will find out who killed our precious darlings."'

Chapter Three

Faro stared at Brown in stunned silence.

Should he feel flattered? Was he actually being asked . . . ? Nay, the Queen didn't ask, she commanded, and he was being commanded to investigate disappearing dogs that got themselves shot.

In constant danger of losing the crown off her Royal head by wandering unconcerned within the sights of madmen's guns, the centre of sinister plots emanating from a dozen different European countries, here she was demanding that the deaths of two household pets be investigated by Scotland's prime detective.

He had a sudden desire to laugh out loud at the absurdity of the task. At the same time he was seized by a considerable eagerness that none of his colleagues in Edinburgh's Central Office should ever be made aware that Faro was now searching for dog-killers. Even Royal dog-killers.

Brown stroked his beard, regarding Faro's silence thoughtfully. 'Too difficult for ye, Inspector?'

Faro pulled himself together with some effort. 'I shouldn't think so. But I thought it was the Crathie murder you wanted to discuss.'

Brown opened his mouth, closed it again. 'And why should I want to discuss that in particular?' he demanded suspiciously.

'I am a detective, sir,' Faro replied trying not to respond with the indignation Brown's questions warranted.

'That matter is closed. The lass is dead and buried. No one knows who killed her. Person or persons unknown. That was the verdict.'

He put heavy emphasis on the last word and continued sternly, 'I have been directed here, Inspector, by the Queen to bring to your attention the matter of her twa dogs.'

'What kind of dogs were they?' Faro asked repressing a sigh.

'King Charles spaniels. Peaceful brutes, if that's what ye're getting at, Inspector. No' the kind to threaten any puir body. Or take a nip out o' a passing ankle. No' like some,' he said with a dark look at his bare leg on which a closer inspection might have revealed a profusion of ancient scars suspiciously like those of canine encounters.

Faro nodded. King Charles spaniels. How like Royalty. 'What were their names?' If he had to conduct a murder enquiry presumably Royal dogs merited the same methods as mortal victims.

Brown thought for a moment. His frown deemed this a somewhat unnecessary question. 'Er, Dash and – Flash. Aye, that's it. Grand at following the guns.'

Faro considered this statement. And no doubt it was the most likely cause of their unfortunate end. He pictured them growing stout like their Royal mistress, slow-moving. Too slow-moving to get out of the way of exuberant grouse-shooters.

'Male or female?'

Brown thought about that too. 'Och, we dinna worry. There's always more men than wummin, ye ken.'

'I beg your pardon. I meant the dogs, not the guns.'

'Och, man, you should have said what ye meant,' was the reprimand.

'Dogs or bitches, we call them. These twa were bitches.' And with a defiant stare, 'And no' in heat, if that's what ye're getting at.'

Faro was disappointed at this deflation of his second

31

logical conclusion for the disappearance of bitches. 'Shot by mistake obviously. Got too close to the birds. Or the sheep,' he added lamely.

Brown shook his head. 'No,' he said firmly. 'I havena' told the Queen, I didna' want to upset the puir lady but they were shot through the head. And from the powder burns I'd say at very close range.'

'Where and when were they discovered, Mr Brown?'

'Twa hundred yards from the Castle. On the path by the river. Night after the Ghillies' Ball.'

The estate was vast, thought Faro despairingly. The dogs buried and nearly two weeks later, there would be few clues, that was for sure.

Regarding Faro sternly, Brown continued. 'Look, man, all this isna' of much importance. It's no' where it happened, the Queen wants to know. We all ken that. It is who would deliberately shoot the Queen's favourite dogs.'

It was at this stage of the conversation that Faro decided that Brown, excellent fellow though he was, would never make a detective. The first question was 'Where and when?' Which almost inevitably led to the second, 'Why?' and lastly, the all-important 'Who?' For in that sequence lay hidden the precise clues to the killer's identity.

Early in his career Faro had hit upon the almost infallible theory that the criminal inevitably leaves behind from his person some tangible piece of evidence, be it a thread of torn clothing, a footprint, or some small possession lost in the death struggle which might be used to link him with his victim. And in the same manner, he reasoned, the murderer also carried away on his person by accident some substance identifiable with either the victim or the scene of the crime.

This theory had rarely let him down in his twenty years with the Edinburgh City Police. He held it in such high regard that he saw no good reason to abandon it when considering dogs instead of humans.

'I should like to see the exact spot, if you please.'

Brown shrugged. 'They are buried in the pets' cemetery, among all the wee birds, dogs and horses that have served the Queen loyally. She is sentimental about such things—'

'You mistake my meaning, Mr Brown,' Faro interrupted. 'I wish to see where the dogs were found.'

Brown regarded him a little contemptuously. 'As you wish, Inspector. But take my word for it, there's nothing there. Ye'll be wasting your time.'

'Nevertheless,' said Faro firmly.

'Verra well, verra well. If you insist. And it's a fair walk – Inspector,' he added in the pitying tone reserved for the born countryman's idea of the town-bred traveller.

'And I'm a fair walker, Mr Brown. You have to be in my job, you know, tracking down criminals.'

Brown seemed surprised at this information. He responded by nodding vigorously and withdrawing a handsome gold timepiece from his waistcoat pocket, 'It'll need to be the morning then. I'm on duty at the Castle within the hour.'

'Tomorrow it is, then.' Faro walked with Brown to the gate. 'I am about to visit my aunt in the hospital at Beagmill.'

'Beagmill.' Brown smiled. 'Lachlan has the trap at the road end, so if you'd care to accompany us, we'll set you down there.'

Glancing down at his boots, hastily retied, Faro bowed. 'My feet are obliged to you, sir.'

Brown gave him a sympathetic nod and Faro added, 'Is there room for Dr Laurie?'

'I dinna see why not.'

Faro signalled to Vince who was staring out of the window. And as they walked ahead of him on to the roadway, Brown was unable to suppress his curiosity. 'Yon's a fair dainty young man.'

'My stepson, sir.'

Brown seemed surprised. 'A real physician, is he?' His tone implied awe.

'He is indeed. He takes up the post of locum tenens at your hospital tomorrow.'

'Well, well.' John Brown didn't greet this information with any enthusiasm. 'He looks awfa' young. No more than a bairn.'

'I warn you not to be misled by appearances, sir. He's a good man to have around in a fight, I assure you. And what is more, he is my most trusted assistant. His help has been invaluable in solving many of my most difficult cases.'

'Do you say so? Well, I never.' Brown's response implied disbelief and Faro glancing back realised from the scarlet colour that flooded Vince's ears that he had overheard Brown's hoarse whisper.

He looked at his stepfather and mouthed indignantly, 'Of all the nerve.'

As they walked down the steep hill to where Lachlan and the dog-cart waited, with a desperate need to change the subject, Faro asked, 'Is Lachlan your son?'

'Nay, Inspector. I'm not wed. He's a fostered bairn wi' one o' my cousins. Been away at the college, studying.' He made it sound a formidable task.

As they boarded the cart, he continued, 'Brown's a common name hereabouts. From the days when the clans were proscribed and the laird's kin took something a little less dangerous than their Gaelic surnames . . .'

Clattering wheels and the bumpy texture of the steep track made further conversation impossible. The scenery however was enchanting and Faro was quite content to gaze at the panorama of mountain and stream and breathe in the wine-clear air, already sharpened like his appetite by the hint of autumn waiting in the wings.

Far above their heads another flash of gold.

'Yon's a golden eagle, Inspector. Has his eyrie on Craig Gowan.'

The eagle soared, the sunlight on widespread wings

turning him into that bird of fiction, a phoenix rising. Along the line of the mountains rose sharp triangles of stone. Brown followed Vince's gaze.

'Cairns, doctor,' said Brown in answer to his question. 'Monuments put up by Her Majesty to mark some memorable event in her family's stay at Balmoral. Yon's Beagmill.'

Lachlan reined in the cart opposite a handsome granite building set back from the road.

'Until tomorrow, then, gentlemen. We will look by for you at nine.'

Faro and Vince walked up the drive to the main door. Embedded in stone letters: 'The Prince Consort Cottage Hospital. 1860.' Inside a wooden board with a Royal coat of arms declared the establishment 'dedicated to the alleviation and treatment of illness and disease among Her Majesty's loyal servants and tenants'.

The hospital had two strictly separate wings, whose entrances bore the words 'Men' and 'Women' also carved indelibly in stone, the sexes sharply and properly divided.

Although undeniably small, Faro observed that the wards were a considerable improvement on the housing conditions prevailing in many a Scottish town.

For the poor of Edinburgh's High Street with their squalid tenements and wynds supporting ten of a family in one dreadful room, such cleanliness and orderly comfort would have prompted thoughts that they had died and gone to heaven.

Prince Albert's main concern had been the health of the young: too many infants died at birth or succumbed to the many diseases of infancy. Among Britain's poor, to have survived forty years was to have reached old age, and many were consigned to earlier graves by neglected illness and hard work. Ironic, was the whisper, that for all his good works, the Prince had died at forty-two of typhoid and, some hinted, of medical mismanagement.

A decade later, residents were either extremely healthy or regarded hospitals with suspicion. Wards were rarely

more than one quarter filled and patients fell into categor-
ies of broken limbs, amputations (through horrendous
accidents with farm equipment) but rarely the old and
infirm.

The latter were something of a rarity, usually incomers
or foreigners to the district, since hardy local folk never
gave up, and old Balmoral servants preferred to die in
Royal harness. Or in extremities of age, they drifted into
a happy second childhood under the careful and loving
attention of the younger members of the family.

The Prince had provided the hospital with a doctor and
three nurses. He had liked his doctors to be young and
imaginative, perhaps even a little rebellious in the cause
of medical progress. The present incumbent, who was
approaching his seventieth year, had been prevailed upon
to take a short holiday and to employ a young assistant.

While Vince's Dundee appointment as factory doctor
eminently qualified him for such responsibility, the un-
happiness in his personal life had also taken toll of
his never-abundant self-confidence. He had it on good
authority, however, that should he prove worthy of the
hospital appointment and Dr Elgin's esteem, then he
might be offered a permanency.

Was it the Balmoral connection that attracted Vince,
a step nearer his ultimate dream, the goal of Queen's
physician, Faro wondered. He entertained some mis-
givings about his young stepson hiding himself away in
a country hospital instead of a large town where he could
gain experience and expertise in medical diagnoses.

The hospital seemed ideal for a family man, a middle-
aged doctor and a countryman at heart, rather than a
young man at the beginning of his profession. Vince,
Faro suspected, would soon become bored.

'Dr Elgin,' the nurse-in-charge informed Vince sternly,
'was not expecting your arrival until tomorrow. He is now
off duty for the evening and is only available in case of an
emergency.'

'Then please do not disturb him on my account. I have lodging for the night and will present myself tomorrow.'

Consulting notes on the desk, the nurse said, 'Not before eleven, if you please. Eleven o'clock is when Dr Elgin completes his morning rounds,' she added, directing them to the ward where Aunt Bella received them rapturously with hugs and kisses.

At last all three, rather damp about the eyes, settled back and with assurances that Bella would be home in time for her birthday, they smiled at each other as happily as the stern hospital atmosphere would allow.

The only other occupant of the ward was an old lady with a bandaged head who seemed to be asleep.

'That's Nessie Brodie. It was her cottage burned down. Puir soul,' whispered Bella. 'Ye ken her, Jeremy?'

Faro did vaguely. His aunt would enjoy having a sympathetic companion and a captive audience. For if that blameless lady had a solitary fault it was being a compulsive talker.

Talk was to her like breathing. The house resounded with ceaseless chatter between Tibbie and Bella, though Faro suspected that neither heard one half of what the other was saying. And on the rare occasions when Bella thought she had the house to herself, she was quite happy keeping her vocal chords in excellent trim by talking to herself.

Now her sole disappointment at going home was the knowledge that her beloved great-nephew was to be Dr Elgin's assistant.

'If that isna' an awfa' coincidence,' she cried. 'And me not to be here to keep an eye on ye.'

The old woman in the next bed stirred, muttered something and closed her eyes again.

'Puir Nessie, she's no' been the same since the night I dragged her out of the fire.' Faro and Vince listened patiently, unwilling to tell her that Tibbie had already stolen her drama in the detailed account of the cottage in flames and Bella's daring rescue.

37

'Och, I'm just fine,' she assured them cheerfully. 'Ma legs are still bandaged, ye ken, but I'm getting on grand. Just a few scratches.'

With a sigh, she continued: 'They wouldna' consider letting me bide in ma' own home. Said I was to come into the hospital where I could be looked after properly. Ma stairs are a wee thing steep and narrow, and puir Tibbie's no' able to heave me up and down. Lassie's that frail hersel'.'

'You were very lucky, Auntie,' Faro said.

Her smile was pure content. 'The Good Lord looks after his own. I have every faith that ma prayers will be answered and I'll be home for ma birthday.' And with a tender look, 'I prayed that ye would manage to come as well, Jeremy lad. And Vince too. I am blessed. It wouldna' be the same without you. If only your dear mother and the wee bairns—'

She listened to Faro's explanation with concern. 'Those puir wee lambs. Let's hope they dinna have their bonny faces marked—'

'No, dear. That's smallpox not chicken-pox.'

That assurance came from Vince and she looked at him gratefully. 'Afore I forget, Jeremy, ye'll be sad to hear—'

There followed a gloomy recapitulation of all the people who had died since Faro's last visit. Again he listened, holding her hand and squeezing it encouragingly as he put in the occasional exclamations of concern that were required of him.

This splendid show of interest was quite beyond Vince whose face, except when Bella's glance fell upon him, set in an attitude of confusion and growing despondency.

But Faro was prepared to be patient. One casual question was guaranteed to bring forth full life histories for the whole district. With Aunt Bella he knew that he had on hand a fount of more valuable information than Inspector Purdie, with headquarters at the Crathie

Inn, walking or riding up miles of farm roads with his exhaustive enquiries would gain in a whole week of painstaking detection.

'What about this murder, Auntie?' Faro asked.

'I was just coming to that. Kin to Nessie, the puir lass,' she said rather loudly.

This had the required effect. As if awaiting her cue, Nessie opened her eyes, looked at the two men and struggled into a sitting position, picking up the conversation with such alacrity that Faro wondered how much she had already overheard.

'Aye, Mr Faro. An awfa' tragedy. Ye ken, the lassie was my niece,' she added dramatically.

'Only by marriage, Nessie,' said Bella sternly, as if resenting this rôle of importance bestowed on her neighbour. 'Nessie, as ye'll recall, used to be an upper servant at the Castle—'

'Aye, and ever since I retired I've been sewing for the Queen, petticoats, and alterations to her gowns.'

'And she's good at it too,' said Bella, reluctant to relinquish her part in the story.

'Had to be, Bella. Especially as the Queen's grown stouter and it's been no easy matter keeping in step with all the extra inches without drawing her attention to it.'

'One would have assumed that the Royal coffers would run to new linen for such a contingency,' said Vince.

'True, true. But the Queen is well known to have her head turned fast against wastefulness.'

Faro suppressed a smile. It was common knowledge from his experiences at the Palace of Holyroodhouse, that she kept a tight hold on the Royal purse strings.

'Anyway, getting stout would depress the poor lady, especially as she likes her food—'

'And her drink too, I hear,' said Bella in a cautious whisper. 'After all, she hasna' much else to console her, puir lady, being a widow and having sic' responsibilities.'

'You were telling us about this unfortunate lass,' said Faro in a kindly but determined effort to direct the conversation.

Nessie frowned. 'From Aberdeen way. Must have been on Dave's side o' the family. He left home when he was thirteen, and I was fair flabbergast when Morag walked in six months ago. Or was it seven. Let me see—'

With Bella's help this was at last sorted out to Nessie's satisfaction. The flow of duelling words was interrupted by a nurse with the information for Dr Laurie that Dr Elgin had learned of his unexpected arrival and would be delighted to receive him.

Vince accompanied her willingly, kissing his great-aunt and promising to take care of both patients.

Goodbyes were said and Faro, looking at the momentarily speechless ladies, urged them on: 'You were saying. About Morag. Do go on.'

Nessie needed no further encouragement. 'Seems she was orphaned long since and had found some letters. When she saw that we lived on Balmoral Estate, she had heard so much about Ballater being a great place for holidays, she decided to see if she could get work in one of the hotels. She came to me first, and I did better than that for her.

'Bonny, a wee bittie wild, but I kenned they were needing kitchen servants at the Castle and Johnnie Brown put in a word for her. He took a right shine to the lass. So did Lachlan.'

Pausing, she sighed. 'We all had hopes there. And we were, well, surprised when she told us she was to marry a footman.'

Suddenly she began to cry. 'It's awful, awful. I can hardly believe it. I blame myself, Mr Faro. Really I do. When she didn't come home, I thought nothing of it. She was often kept late at the Castle. And now for this to happen. I canna believe such wickedness.'

'Murdered,' Bella said to Faro. 'Stabbed she was. Body found over Crathie way, in a ditch. Just up past the signpost to Tomintoul.' She sighed. 'Twa-three days after she nearly drowned, too—'

'I was coming to that, Bella,' Nessie interrupted reproachfully. 'Aye, it wasna' the first time that devil had it in for puir Morag. When she was crossing over on the Abergeldie cradle wi' her footman – the quickest way o' getting to Crathie, all the servants use it,' she explained to Faro – 'they both fell into the water.'

'Everyone was a bit fu', ye ken,' said Bella, 'but Brown's laddie dived in and saved her. Puir James—'

'The footman, Jimmy Lessing,' put in Nessie.

'Oh, he was drowned, puir laddie,' Bella continued rapidly, in case this interruption should divert the telling of the tale to her companion. 'His body smashed to bits at the mill race. Terrible it was. Terrible.'

'And our puir Morag only knew him from the ring she'd given him—'

'Dreadful, dreadful,' said Faro sympathetically.

'Then Nessie's cottage burnt down,' said Bella, her voice heavy with significance. 'The night after the Ghillies' Ball.'

'A Saturday it was. I hadna' seen Morag that week. She mostly came by on a Thursday to bring me the Queen's sewing, or she'd look in on a Saturday for a wee chat. But she never came that week at all.' Nessie sounded bewildered, her voice fretful with anxiety.

'I'd never ha' managed the twa o' ye the night o' the fire,' said Bella. 'But as luck would have it Morag wasna' there.'

Faro felt cynical about luck being involved. It seemed that the girl had been singularly unlucky. Even through the frantic retelling of the story pieced together by the two women, his mind worked fast sifting the unimportant from the significant.

'I ken one thing fine,' Bella said mysteriously. 'The lass was probably expecting. Matters are different in the country. Nature will have its way wi' young folk. I used to be a nursemaid and I ken what I'm talking about. Most marriages hereabouts are from necessity. With so little siller about couples tend to delay until there's a bairn on the way. No one thinks ony the worse of a lass for that. Except the Queen, of course.'

'What has the Queen to do with it?'

'She's that firm and respectable, lad. Covering up the legs of the piano and talking about a limb of chicken or lamb. Maids and footmen are no' supposed to meet in the grounds either. That wasna' much help to poor Morag, bless her.'

'He'll try it again,' said Nessie. Her voice suddenly excited, she put her hands to her face. 'They'll get her yet. And she'll no listen to anyone. Morag knew. She told me,' she shouted and stabbing a finger in Faro's direction began to sob noisily.

'Nessie, Nessie, dinna' take on so,' said Bella and to Faro she whispered, 'Tak' no heed of her, puir tormented soul. It's that dunt on the head did it to her. She has nightmares. Thinks someone's trying to harm the Queen, but no one will believe her.'

Faro felt an ominous chill at the words. He regarded the patient in the other bed thoughtfully, alarmed at the sudden change from normal conversation into hysterical denunciation. Perhaps her mind was wandering. That must surely be the medical and the logical explanation.

But – was it? Was there something far more sinister, a link between the killing of the pet dogs and the girl who called regularly at Nessie's house to deliver the Queen's sewing?

Was he on the threshold of a plot of much greater magnitude, one that might threaten the life of the Queen herself?

But there was no possibility of further questioning. Nessie's head had sunk on to her chest and the bell for the end of visiting hour having already rung, he gave his aunt a farewell hug.

In the entrance hall he saw Vince, now accompanied

by Dr Elgin, whose rotund figure and rosy complexion testified to good living and belied his seventy summers.

He greeted Faro with a charming friendliness that must have been a boon to his patients.

'We have a room in readiness for Dr Laurie.'

'And an early start tomorrow,' said Vince.

'Six o'clock,' added Dr Elgin cheerfully.

Faro saw Vince's eyes roll heavenward. A sluggish riser, he was never at his best in the early morning.

'Since your time with us is short, Mr Faro, we must spare Dr Laurie to you as often as we can.'

'Thank you, sir.'

Then he added, 'Perhaps you would care to join us for a little light refreshment before we retire.'

'Thank you, no, sir. It has been a long day.'

As Faro tactfully made his excuses, Dr Elgin said, 'Please feel at liberty to visit your aunt whenever you wish. Our strict visiting hours do not apply to such an illustrious visitor.' He smiled. 'You have my permission to ignore them. I shall tell the staff that you are to be admitted at any time.'

At the door he added, 'You have a vehicle to take you back to Easter Balmoral?'

'Alas, no. But I am used to walking.'

Faro, acutely aware of his new boots, was grateful when Dr Elgin continued, 'May I recommend the livery stables a hundred yards down the road. Willie keeps late hours and as the season is almost over, he may be able to accommodate you.'

Thanking him, Faro left the hospital feeling much happier about Vince's prospects. He was sure there would be a rapport between the two doctors. Suddenly conscious of how tired he was, footsore and weary, the prospect of hiring a pony-trap for a few days seemed an excellent idea.

At the stables the 'pony' turned out to be an ex-race-horse.

'He used to be a good runner in the Abergeldie stables

in his prime, belonged to the Prince of Wales,' said Willie proudly, explaining that he had been a jockey in his young days. 'We've both got too old for that, of course, but should you care to ride, there's a saddle. He's a biddable beast, ye ken.' And patting the horse's head affectionately, 'There's only one thing, sir, he needs stabling, a proper night's lodging.'

'There's a barn at Mistress MacVae's—'

'I ken it fine. There'll be no problem there,' said the stableman, throwing a bag of oats into the cart and giving Faro full instructions on the care of this valuable animal, whose name it seemed was 'Steady'. Or had he misheard, Faro wondered, when at first it refused to 'Trot on' as instructed.

By the time they had reached Aunt Bella's cottage, however, Faro and his new companion had achieved a brisk pace plus a mutual respect and understanding. Steady seemed to have no complaints on being introduced to his new stabling and blew into Faro's ear affectionately.

Faro slept well that night, and welcomed the almost forgotten sensations of waking sleepily to cock-crow, bird song and warring blackbirds outside the window. Even the raucous din of a full-going rookery was music to his ears.

As he opened the casement window, distant sounds emerged, sheep bleating on the hill, indistinguishable from the white boulders, and a dainty herd of hinds following their lord and master down to the stream to drink.

He sighed with pleasure. If only life could be always like this, if he could keep this moment and carry it with him like a letter, or a faded rose. For these scenes thrust him back vividly into the days of his childhood, now almost obliterated by years of city life.

Breathing deeply, he filled his lungs with the pure air and hurried downstairs, lured by the appetising smells of cooking.

Tibbie was taking bannocks out of the oven. She smiled a greeting and as he sat down at the table with sunshine flooding the room, life seemed very good indeed.

It could be perfect, he decided, if only people stopped murdering one another.

Chapter Four

At the hospital he found Vince awaiting his arrival. Dr Elgin had been good to his promise and with few patients to attend, he had been given the morning off.

Impressed and relieved to see his stepfather equipped with a pony-trap, he said, 'How clever of you. And invaluable in the circumstances. Should keep you one trot ahead and save wearing out the precious boot-leather. He moves faster who has a horse and cart.'

'He also moves faster who can ride.' And as they set off Faro related Willie's tale of Steady's distinguished early days.

They had reached Abergeldie Castle when Vince said, 'We will certainly be in good time for John Brown – perhaps even for a couple of Tibbie's excellent bannocks before he arrives,' he added wistfully.

Faro smiled. 'How's it going, lad? Settling in all right?'

'Yes, indeed, Stepfather. You know I think I'm really going to enjoy being here. Food apart.' He sighed. 'Dr Elgin is a splendid fellow, such stories to tell. You should have stayed to supper,' he added reproachfully. 'You would hardly credit what medicine used to be like in the old days. Makes me thankful I didn't take it up before the advent of chloroform. A course in butchery would have been more useful than a medical training.'

His mood had turned sombre. Clinging to his seat as they negotiated the sharp bend, he asked, 'About this murder, Stepfather. Aren't you intrigued?'

Faro related the version he had gathered from Nessie and Bella. At the end, Vince frowned.

'A rum do, I'd call it, Stepfather. And everyone very keen to get the corpse off stage and the enquiry closed as quickly as possible. The fact that Lachlan Brown was sweet on the girl may be of some significance.'

'My thoughts exactly.'

John Brown was already waiting for them outside the cottage, the silent Lachlan at his side, whose presence Faro now considered with more attention than at their first meeting.

Impressed by the Inspector's enterprise in arranging his own transport, Brown nodded approvingly. 'If ye'll just follow us, then.'

The estate grounds were vast and towards the main drive, with a glimpse of the Royal residence across wide lawns, Lachlan led the way down a narrow path through the trees.

In sight of the river, they alighted and walked to the path where only a footfall away, the Dee sparkled and burbled on its way to the German Ocean.

Brown pointed with his foot to a stone. 'That's where we found the dogs.'

Vince and Faro immediately crouched down to make a careful study of the area, parting the grass and examining it carefully. Brown watched this procedure with wide-eyed astonishment. To Faro's question he replied: 'Aye, this was exactly the spot. Isn't that so?'

Lachlan, so addressed, merely nodded. Silent and withdrawn, Faro was beginning to wonder whether the lad was shy or had some vocal handicap.

'Did it rain, by any chance, on the night the dogs disappeared?'

Brown thought about that. 'No, not that night. But we had a storm the night before.'

'And there has been no rain since?'

'Nary a drop. A dry spell is usual for this time of year.'

So the low water in the river had indicated. Faro was pleased with this accurate timing. There should have been imprinted on the dried mud paw marks, bloodstains and tufts of dog hair.

There were none.

The grass was undisturbed. No scuffle marks, no bruised grass, nothing to suggest that the dogs had been resting and had been surprised by their killer.

Faro stood up, certain of one thing: that they had been killed elsewhere and their bodies carried to this spot for discovery.

But why?

Brown meanwhile watched the antics of the two men as if they had taken leave of their senses. Consulting his watch gravely, he said, 'I must leave you, gentlemen.'

Vince had walked a little distance away, stepping through a tangle of weeds to what had once been a handsome watermill, now falling into neglect and crumbling ruin.

'Ye'll no' find anything there, doctor,' Brown called after him. 'It's here the puir beasts were killed.' And to Faro, 'I'll tell the Queen that ye're looking into it, conducting an enquiry. Isn't that what ye call it?'

And with a flicker of amusement as Faro bowed in assent and made to follow Vince, 'That hasna' been used since the new mill was built the Crathie side o' the river. The Queen bought the miller's land here to add to the estate.'

'Was it intended for some useful purpose?'

Brown looked up at the empty windows. 'It was just in the way, ye ken. Untidy-looking. Buying it was almost the last thing Prince Albert did before he died. And somehow Her Majesty hadna' heart to do anything about it after that. Like everything else, it was left to lie exactly as it was on the day when she and Prince Albert looked it over together and decided to buy it.'

Moving towards the path again he said, 'I'll need to go, Inspector.' Pointing to the pony-trap, he added, 'No need for ye to spend yer money on that. Tell Willie ye need it for yer investigations and the Queen will pay the bill.'

'I'm most obliged to Her Majesty for her generosity.' Faro had already decided that the Royal task he had been set was doomed to failure and with it, any hopes he had been cherishing of a quiet fishing holiday.

'Before you go, Mr Brown. Have there been any similar incidents reported?'

'In what way similar?'

'Anything like this business. Violent deeds, damage to property,' he said helpfully.

Brown scratched his beard, frowning. 'Let me see. There was the fire at Mistress Brodie's croft. But that was an accident. The puir woman is in the hospital—'

'Yes, I met her last night.'

Brown frowned. 'That was how your auntie got injured, ye'll ken that. Nothing mysterious about it. Barns often go on fire.'

'What about the murder of Morag Brodie? Did that not raise a stir in the neighbourhood?' The question seemed superfluous. In a rural community, if his Aunt Bella was a typical resident, no one would be speaking of anything else for months to come.

Lachlan was very still and when Brown replied, he did so reluctantly. 'Aye, the lass who got herself killed.'

And Faro, thinking that was a curious way to express it, as if Morag Brodie had deserved death, asked, 'Where was her body found?'

'In a ditch over yonder. Crathie way.' Brown's eyes slid across Lachlan. 'That case is closed.'

'A murder without a murderer, whatever the verdict, is never closed as far as I'm concerned, Mr Brown.'

Brown looked him straight in the eyes. 'But then ye're not concerned, are ye, Inspector?' he fairly crowed. 'And Detective Inspector Purdie – from Scotland Yard,' he added significantly, 'is satisfied with the verdict.'

'I understood that the lass was a servant at the Castle?'

'How did ye guess that?' Brown's glance was suspicious,

49

and although his question was chilly, it was asked with elaborate carelessness.

'I didn't. My aunt was full of it, of course.'

Brown's sigh of relief was audible as he once more glanced at the silent sullen Lachlan. 'I must awa'. If you want any more information about – about Morag Brodie, why d'ye no' ask the Inspector. Or Sergeant Whyte, our local lad.'

The moment of danger was past; he was prepared to be affable, even expansive. 'Detective Inspector Purdie is acquainted with these parts. Like yeself he used to bide here for holidays when he was a wee lad.'

Turning to leave, he came back. Facing Faro squarely, hands on hips, he said, 'Ye should know, Inspector, that we're trying to keep all this business from the Queen. As much as possible. We dinna want to distress her.'

His voice defiant, he added, 'It must be obvious to ye that we do our best to give her a restful holiday and spare her as much as possible from anything sordid or unhappy.'

Or anything concerned with the real world, Faro added silently. A brutal murder would obviously tarnish her vision of Balmoral as the 'dear Paradise' she and her beloved Prince Consort had built.

'We are proud to have Her Majesty at Balmoral and we like to keep her happy and content with us. This is her only place now where she feels at home. It's her refuge. We dinna want to spoil that for her.' It was quite a speech. 'The puir woman has had that much grief,' he added desperately.

But Faro was unmoved. Considerably less grief than most of her subjects, he thought bitterly. And surely the Queen should be more concerned about the possibility of a murderer living in the midst of her rustic tenantry than the unfortunate death of two pet dogs, however beloved.

Neither man spoke. Observing Faro's guarded expression, Brown moved unhappily from one foot to the other.

Then consulting his watch, he looked over his shoulder towards the Castle. Touching his bonnet briefly, he took Lachlan by the arm and walked rapidly in the direction of the Royal apartments.

Faro watched them go, his mind on Morag Brodie.

'Stepfather. Over here.' Vince waved to him excitedly from one of the upstairs windows of the ruined mill.

Faro picked his way through thorn and briar that would have done justice to the Sleeping Beauty's Palace and did nothing for his trousers and coat, or his temper. Opening the creaking door into shuttered semi-darkness, he shivered.

As his eyes became accustomed to the gloom he saw that this had once been the kitchen. The heart of family life, it had known laughter and prosperity. Now the sense of desolation rushed out, clawing at him. Cheerless and forbidding, it was not a place in which he would care to linger. And although it was still sturdily roofed, he would have no wish to seek its sanctuary on a stormy night.

Vince gazed down at him.

'Up here, Stepfather.'

'Found something, lad?' said Faro climbing the open staircase.

'Yes, look around you. What do you make of this?'

Signs of domesticity, blankets and sheets, even a table-cloth, two mugs and plates, and a vase of wilted flowers indicated that this room had been recently occupied.

'And over here,' said Vince. 'Bloodstains.'

Faro studied the marks on the floorboards. He could see a dark area at the top of the stairs, which continued downwards, streaks on steps and stone walls. Bending down, he picked up a small clump of brown hair.

'From the dogs?'

'Perhaps, Stepfather. And on the bed. Spaniels shed a lot of hair. I would hazard a guess that they were both shot in here and their bodies carried out to the river path.'

Pausing Vince looked around the room. 'Are you thinking the same as I am, Stepfather?'

'Precisely. That this place has been lived in recently. And by someone who was no passing stranger seeking shelter. And no tinker. Tinkers care little for sheets and fine blankets. They don't put flowers in vases, either.'

'But girls do. Especially girls who are entertaining a lover.'

'Ah, now we're getting somewhere, lad,' said Faro as he examined the fireplace. 'Let us reconstruct the scene. This was a clandestine meeting. No fire was lit, for that would bring attention to the fact that the ruined mill had an occupant. The bedlinen and tablecloth indicate a lass of refined taste.'

Considering for a moment, he said, 'I think if we gathered these together and took them to the Castle, we would find they originated from the same source in the linen room. Purloined by Morag Brodie for the special occasion which, alas, was to cost her her life.'

'So you think she stayed here.'

'Undoubtedly. She spent the night she was killed here and perhaps one night before. But no more than that.'

'How can you tell?'

'Fine linen sheets like these crease badly and have to be changed frequently. Consider their almost pristine condition. And the two pillowcases, lad. Only one has been used. I would say that only Morag slept here and that she waited in vain for her lover. And when he finally arrived, it was not to sleep with her, but to put a knife in her.'

Faro wandered back to the stairhead. 'But not in the bed,' he said. And eying the scene narrowly, 'Probably here. Where the blood has soaked into the floorboards. But for some reason it was inconvenient to dispose of her body, and while he was awaiting his chance the Queen's inquisitive dogs came on the scene. He realises his danger, shoots them and carries their bodies on to the river path. Does this suggest anything to you?'

'Only that the murderer might have been someone employed at the Castle. A fellow-servant?'

'Or a ghillie,' was the reply.

'And if your theory is correct, Stepfather, he is still lurking about, his crime undetected. Another good reason for not spreading alarm and despondency in the Royal apartments.'

'And for apprehending him before he strikes again. In the light of our discovery, I think it might be prudent to look in at the local police station. See what new material, if any, Inspector Purdie has come upon.'

There was a moment's silence before Vince said gently, 'Stepfather, I thought I heard you say that Superintendent McIntosh had warned you off.'

'Indeed yes, but perhaps the good Inspector will have something to offer on the subject of murdered dogs,' said Faro innocently. 'But first of all we must return you to the hospital and pay our respects to Aunt Bella.'

'It is as well you have Dr Elgin's blessing. I was given to understand most firmly that visiting times are strictly adhered to, despite the current lack of patients.'

As they drove briskly in the direction of the cottage hospital, Faro was silent, his mind still exploring the scene they had left behind at the ruined mill.

'More theories?' Vince asked, finally breaking the silence. 'About the dogs, I mean?'

'One is at a considerable disadvantage not to have had a sight of the bodies. The murdered girl and the dogs all neatly buried. Having to take it all on hearsay is very inconvenient. And irritating.'

'Taken that all we were told of the discovery of the dogs was correct,' said Vince. He had concluded that Brown would be a reliable witness and, in common with his stepfather, a man who could be guaranteed to miss little. 'It has just occurred to me – might not slaying the Queen's pet dogs rate as a treasonable crime?'

'Indeed, yes. Damage to her personal property, lèse-majesté and so forth would undoubtedly merit a heavy jail sentence.'

'And one she would see to personally, I don't doubt,

and the Royal displeasure is enough to strike terror into the heart of any prospective dog-slayer,' said Vince.

'That makes sense, lad, but let's consider what doesn't. Why go to all that trouble, leaving the bodies around? Why not just bury them, throw them into the river, or carry them across the river in that excellent and convenient cradle? Dispose of them well away from the scene of the crime as no doubt was the case with the murdered girl?'

'That thought had occurred to me, Stepfather. Perhaps their killer was interrupted in the act—'

Faro made an impatient gesture. 'Do not let us miss the real point. We have built up a picture of what we think might have happened. But why? For if the dogs' deaths are coincidental and unconnected with the girl's murder, although the timing would seem to indicate the contrary, what else could they have done to merit death?'

'Not everyone is fond of dogs. Perhaps they made a nuisance of themselves. Took nips out of the servants,' Vince suggested.

'Vince, these are the Queen's pets. For the servants, having nips taken out of their ankles would be an occupational hazard.' Faro sucked in his lip. 'There was only one reason. A threat to the murderer's safety. That is the only logical reason why anyone would go to the extent of incurring Her Majesty's extreme displeasure – and we can all guess the consequences of that. Remember. You cannot blackmail a dog,' he continued. 'Perhaps they knew their killer and he panicked.'

Vince thought for a moment. 'Let's suppose that a farmer had shot them for sheep worrying, for instance. Then he wouldn't have carried them back here, Royal collars and all, as a mark of defiance, would he?'

'Any farmer who had marauding dogs on his land, Royal or no, would have a legitimate cause for indignation and the assurance that right – and the law – was on his side. But we have Brown's word that these King Charles spaniels were the most docile of animals.'

'Of course, one dog shot could have been an accident.'

'Got in the way of an indifferent gun? True, there are many around at this time of year.'

'That would be a possibility, Stepfather. Especially if he was afraid of the Queen's wrath.'

'But not two dogs, lad. Not shot through the head at point blank range. We are dealing with a much more complex situation here than an irate but scared farmer who didn't see the Royal collars until too late. Or an unlucky sportsman.'

The hospital gates were in sight. As he stepped down, Vince said suddenly, 'Isn't this all a bit far-fetched, Stepfather? After all there could be another simpler, quite coincidental explanation.'

'Then I'd like to hear it. Go on.'

'Well, they could have been sniffing about that mill regularly after rats and scared a poacher who panicked. Nothing to do with Morag Brodie's murder.'

'Let us hope you are right, lad,' said Faro fervently. But he was unable to stifle the growing fear that the murder of Morag Brodie was but a prelude to something much more important their killer had in his sights. And that the dogs had somehow been in danger of revealing all.

As they entered the hospital, approaching them from the direction of the wards were two uniformed policemen and one in plain clothes.

Faro stopped. 'Detective Inspector Purdie, I presume.'

'Indeed, yes.'

'Faro, from Edinburgh City Police.'

'This is a pleasant surprise. Your exploits are well known to us.'

Faro shook hands with the tall, burly detective. His face was luxuriously bearded, and keen eyes regarded him from behind gold-rimmed spectacles. His appearance implied that this would be a good man to have around in a fight.

'Sergeant Whyte of the local constabulary,' said Purdie, indicating the elder of the two who saluted smartly.

'And Sergeant Craig.'

'Extra staff for the duration of Her Majesty's visit,' Whyte put in, indicating that his own seniority was not in dispute.

'Sergeant Craig is here to assist me. I particularly requested someone who has experience of murder investigations and also knows this area.' Purdie's apologetic look in Whyte's direction suggested an awareness of discord between the two officers. The elder and more experienced had obviously been made to feel insecure by this appointment.

Eager to impress, Craig's smile was supercilious. Here was a young man very pleased with himself. Something familiar in his bearing hinted at the ex-soldier, while a new uniform and boots indicated recent promotion. Faro decided Craig was not in any danger of allowing anyone to forget it.

'There isn't much crime in the area, as Sergeant Whyte here will tell you,' said Purdie. 'Normally this case would have been dealt with by Aberdeen.'

'I understood that the case was closed now.'

Purdie eyed him pityingly. 'From my experience, a verdict of murder by person or persons unknown is never satisfactory. Especially with the Queen in residence, every precaution must be taken to ensure her safety. That's why they called in Scotland Yard.'

His shrug was eloquent. It indicated that this was a complete waste of time. 'Dr Laurie tells me your aunt has made a good recovery and she will probably be ready to go home tomorrow. She was looking very fit and cheerful. A great age, but Whyte tells me ninety is not all that unusual for country people. And your aunt still has all her faculties.'

Pausing he smiled. 'She was delighted by the chance of a few words with passing strangers. It was she who told us that Mistress Brodie's important visitors were relatives from Aboyne.'

'You didn't talk to Mistress Brodie then?' asked Vince.

'Alas no, we chose an inconvenient time. When we arrived she already had two persons at her bedside. The nurse implied that this was the limit and a great dispensation outside the official visiting hours.'

'I'm sure we could have arranged—' Vince began.

'Thank you, but I would not dream of disrupting the hospital's routine.' And turning to Faro, 'A stroke of luck meeting you here, Inspector. I have just arrived but when Sergeant Craig told me you were in the area, I could scarcely believe my good fortune.'

Vince, encountering Faro's triumphant look, was saved a reply as a nurse hurried towards him. Bidding them a hasty farewell, he followed her down the corridor.

Faro hesitated a moment, then decided in the circumstances of Purdie and his colleagues having been turned away, it would be tactless to insist upon seeing his aunt.

At the entrance a carriage awaited Purdie. A not-too-cleverly disguised police carriage, which the Inspector from Scotland Yard was important enough to have placed at his disposal. It was, Faro thought, a conveyance calculated to hinder a discreet investigation, alerting every citizen guiltily concealing an illicit still or poacher's trap and sending waves of alarm and despondency into the surrounding district. Its repercussions would undoubtedly be felt even in those areas where law was administered both rarely and reluctantly by the portly, easy-going Sergeant Whyte.

Looking back at the hospital, Purdie said to Craig, 'We will return later.' And to Faro, 'We have delayed it as much as possible until Mistress Brodie was considered fit to respond to our official enquiries about the fire.' He sighed. 'This is the second of our mistimed visits since we linked our endeavours to those of Sergeant Whyte who has failed to make any progress.'

Both men looked at the unfortunate Whyte who shuffled his feet miserably.

'We thought she might be able to throw some light

upon the murdered girl's last hours,' said Purdie. 'Being kin, and so forth.'

Considering whether he should, at this point, reveal his discoveries in the ruined mill, Faro decided to await a more opportune moment. 'My aunt tells me Nessie Brodie has been very muddled since the accident.'

Craig shook his head disapprovingly, and patted his notebook pocket with military precision. 'The first time we found her fast asleep when we looked in. It was Inspector Purdie's decision that we should return later.' His pitying glance conveyed the impression that his superior officer was too soft-hearted by far and that he, Craig, wouldn't have had any hesitation about waking the old woman up.

'After all, this is an official enquiry,' he added to Whyte, creating an impression that the elder policeman was no longer up to his job.

Purdie beamed upon Faro. 'Mistress MacVae was most helpful, Faro, a positive mine of useful information. No doubt you inherited your flair for detection from her.'

It was Faro's turn to smile. He must remember to tell Bella, she would love that.

'We had been toying with a theory that the fire might have been deliberate, perhaps in the mistaken idea that the girl Morag was visiting. However, your aunt told us that Mistress Brodie was well known for her kind heart, allowing tinkers to sleep in her barn and if the weather was bad leaving food and drink there. Just in case any benighted stranger needed shelter or was caught in a storm.'

'Was there a storm on that night?' Faro asked Whyte.

'Not exactly a storm, sir. A fine mist and cold for the time of year—'

'Very well.' And to Craig, 'I presume you have combed thoroughly through the charred ruins.'

'Yes, sir. As a matter of fact Inspector Purdie had a piece of luck. He picked up what looked like a clay pipe.' Craig darted an admiring glance in the Inspector's direction.

Purdie shrugged. 'Doubtless belonged to one of Mistress Brodie's nocturnal visitors. Too many drinks, our tinker fell asleep, pipe in hand, and when he awoke and found he had set the dry hay alight, he panicked and bolted.'

'That's right, sir,' said Whyte triumphantly. 'There are always plenty tinkers about around this time of year. Ghillies' Ball brings them down like vultures, looking for pickings.'

'Have you questioned the tinker camps?' Faro asked.

Whyte looked uncomfortable under the scrutiny of Craig and Purdie.

'They had all gone next morning. Fly-by-nights. And pursuing them is a waste of time. I've had years of it. The sight of a uniform and they either close up like clams or tell a pack of lies.'

Faro sighed. There was a running war between country constables and tinkers who were all too ready to appropriate possessions they regarded as discarded and useless. As this extended to misunderstandings about clothes innocently left to dry on washing lines, the crofters' resentment was understandable.

'About the girl, Morag Brodie. What do the servants she worked with have to say?' he asked Craig.

'They can all account for their movements. First place I checked. Naturally.' Craig sounded mildly indignant at this interrogation.

'Even though Morag was a foreigner by rights,' Whyte intervened, 'the servants found her a sprightly but biddable lass. Only complaint about her I ever heard was a fondness for the bottle. And the lads.'

'Her background has been investigated,' said Craig. 'And everything she told them about herself, which wasn't much, was reliable information. I checked it myself.'

Craig was beginning to sound exasperated and Purdie said patiently, 'These are just the normal routine enquiries after a murder, as I am sure you are aware, Faro.' Pausing he added, 'I don't think you need worry

59

over this one. We're pretty certain we've got our man. A few more loose ends to tie up and I expect to make the arrest within the next day or two.'

'Oh, indeed.' Faro waited hopefully for Purdie to reveal the suspect's name. Instead he merely shook his head mysteriously, without offering any further information.

'I gather you have very few crimes like this one round here,' Faro said to Whyte. 'It must have caused quite a sensation.'

It was Whyte's turn to smile pityingly. 'They're a peaceful lot in these parts, Inspector, not like your city mob. Must be fifty years since the last murder.'

'Were you the first to examine the body?' Faro asked.

'Aye, sir. Jock, from Duncan's farm, found her in the ditch. Came straight for me. Never touched a thing.'

'What were the nature of her injuries?'

'She was stabbed to death, sir.'

'Were there many wounds?'

'No. Just the one.' Whyte touched his chest. 'Just here. Right to the heart. She must have died instantly.'

'Indeed? Now that is very interesting. Tell me, have there been any other incidents in the neighbourhood?'

'What kind of incidents had you in mind, sir?'

'Incidents involving loss of life, let us say.'

Faro realised he was going to have to spell this one out. Giving Whyte time to think, he watched Purdie who, clearly bored with the conversation, was trying to light a pipe. This was no easy task in that unsteady carriage, but one he managed with great expertise and without removing his leather gloves.

'What about the river in spate?' he asked Whyte. 'Doesn't that claim a victim or two? There was a poem I remember when I stayed here as a lad – went something like "Blood-thirsty Dee each year needs three, But Bonny Don, she needs none."'

And to Purdie, 'Perhaps you remember it too.'

Purdie frowned, shook his head while Whyte's response was to regard Faro blankly.

60

Deciding to prompt the sergeant's memory, Faro continued, 'My aunt told me that just a few days before the murder, Morag Brodie was nearly drowned, falling out of the cradle crossing to Crathie. The fellow with her who was drowned was also a servant at the Castle. A footman.'

Whyte looked mutinous and said reproachfully, 'That's all past history, Inspector. Lessing's dead and buried, poor laddie. Nothing to do with the case,' he added huffily.

'We've been all over this ground, Craig and myself. Very carefully, I assure you,' Purdie intervened gently. 'Believe me, we've explored every possible avenue.'

'I do apologise,' said Faro abruptly.

'Not at all, we're delighted to have your keen powers of observation on our side—'

'Now that you ask for it, sir, here is another observation which I am sure has already occurred to you. Is it not strange that the lad who went to the trouble of rescuing her from drowning should have then risked his neck to murder her? I gather from your unspoken comments and other information that has come my way that your prime suspect is Lachlan Brown.'

'That is correct,' said Purdie. 'The Brodie girl had jilted young Brown for the footman who was drowned.'

'Jilting implies that there was talk of marriage.'

Purdie shrugged. 'Country matters, Faro. Let us say rather that the two had been on intimate terms.'

Faro was silent, remembering the evidence of a lovers' assignation in the upstairs room at the mill. With the footman Lessing dead, who else but Lachlan Brown could Morag have been waiting for?

'I should have thought that the answer was rather obvious,' Purdie continued. 'Consider the workings of human nature, if you please. When Brown rescued her and at the same time let her lover drown,' he added emphasising the words, 'he had hopes. When she refused to go back to him, with heaven knows what reproaches,

61

well then, that was that,' he concluded, with an expressive gesture across his throat.

And Faro realised that the Inspector's speculation fitted perfectly his deductions at the mill.

They were in sight of Bella's cottage. 'This is where I leave you,' he said.

A handsome closed carriage stood in the roadway outside the gate.

'Ah,' said Purdie, 'I see you have a visitor.'

Faro shook his head. 'Someone enquiring after my aunt, I expect.'

'We're on our way to Bush Farm. Brown's place.' Purdie paused significantly. 'Bush Farm is very close to where the girl's body was found.'

And as Faro stepped down, he continued, 'I was hoping I might persuade you to accompany us. Take part in a little private investigation, if it would amuse you.'

Faro was tempted but his conscience prevailed. He thought about the Queen's dogs. That was his most urgent priority.

'Perhaps tomorrow, then?'

Inside the cottage was the last person he had expected to see: Superintendent McIntosh patiently awaiting Detective Inspector Faro's arrival.

His presence spelled out one word.

Trouble.

Chapter Five

Superintendent McIntosh dominated the tiny parlour where his huge bulk was being viewed with polite anxiety by Tibbie as he settled uncomfortably, overflowing from one of Bella's diminutive armchairs.

Greeting Faro's entrance with relief, she bobbed a curtsey and hurried into the kitchen with promises of a pot of tea and some fresh pancakes.

Watching the door close, McIntosh said sternly, 'I am here incognito, Faro. This is strictly off the record.' And glancing round the walls nervously as if they might conceal a listener, 'I travelled by carriage from Aberdeen immediately after the wedding—'

A chronicle of trials and tribulations followed, sufficient to convince the uninitiated that in the manner of bees to honey, Superintendent McIntosh attracted disaster.

As for the incognito, Faro thought cynically that a closed carriage outside Bella's cottage would have already become an urgent topic of conversation in every kitchen in Crathie and surrounding areas. The entire populace would now be exchanging theories and speculation about who might be calling on Mistress MacVae. And her away in the hospital.

'I thought it wise not to use the telegraph on this occasion.'

Faro was again grateful for his thoughtfulness, seeing that private messages were an impossibility. All communications were avidly read and their contents subject to endless discussion long before fourth- or fifth-hand they

63

reached their destination. Only those to the Castle under the Queen's personal code were necessarily treated with any reverence.

'It must be something very serious to bring you out of your way, sir.'

McIntosh smiled grimly. 'It is indeed. The wedding made that awful train journey a little easier to bear. The sooner they get that damned Tay Bridge built the better.' He sighed. 'I found myself having to kill two birds with one stone. If you will forgive the inappropriate simile, since it is my most urgent desire to prevent a second bird falling to the gun. A disaster that would be. A national disaster.'

McIntosh was addicted to his mixed metaphors and all Faro could do was listen patiently.

'Do I take it your visit concerns Balmoral and a member of the Royal Family?'

McIntosh seemed astonished that Faro should have made such an obvious deduction. 'Indeed, yes. Her Majesty, Faro, no less. We have just heard from sources at Scotland Yard that there is to be an attempt on her life. Here, before she leaves at the end of the week.'

Faro had a sinking feeling that his intuition had been right. That there was more involved in the servant girl's murder than a jealous lover. It also explained the real reason for the presence of a detective from Scotland Yard.

Two deaths, both conveniently buried and accounted for. Two of the Queen's pet dogs shot. Faro thought rapidly. Could all four put together in the right order add up to the Queen's life in danger?

'About this girl who was murdered. Is there a connection?'

'Highly unlikely.' McIntosh shook his head. 'You're to stay out of that, Faro. I've warned you. They've got Scotland Yard on the case. We must be careful not to create any ill-feeling,' he added nervously.

'I have just made Inspector Purdie's acquaintance.'

64

'Have you indeed? Then remember it's the Queen's safety you are to concentrate on, Faro. There have always been attempts and rumours of attempts. Not only in London either. As you well know, we've been plagued by them in Edinburgh. Fenians with guns, mostly out in the open. This time it is different. This time it is to be an inside job.'

'You mean in the Castle itself?'

'I do. And by someone close, with access to Her Majesty.'

Dear God, the thought made him shudder when he remembered the informality of the daily life at Balmoral. An assassin just had to get lucky once, be in the right place at the right time.

'We have been led to believe that all staff are closely vetted by her security guards.'

McIntosh chortled. 'Captain Tweedie and Captain Dumleigh, known popularly, I understand, as Tweedledum and Tweedledee.'

Faro smiled at this allusion to the instant popularity of Lewis Carroll's sequel to *Alice in Wonderland*, a particular favourite with his two daughters.

'Can you imagine,' McIntosh chortled, 'two big watchful ex-policemen trying hard to look like footmen or pretending to be personal assistants to equerries?'

'Surely all the known Fenians and anarchists have been accounted for? And that last troublesome batch are now safely behind bars.'

'True, Faro, true. We have an excellent secret service in operation and it would be very difficult, given their present sources of reliable information, for any known undesirables to be "slipped" into Balmoral. But this is a new one on us. A domestic assassination.'

Pausing he regarded Faro solemnly. 'The Prince's Party, they call themselves. Recently sprung to our notice. Supposedly they are the staunchest of patriots, their cause the good of England, their message that Queen Victoria neglects her duties and should retire as she is no longer fit to reign over us. She should abdicate and let the Prince of Wales take over the throne.

'They'll go to any lengths, believe me. I'm not saying, between you and me,' he added again with that nervous glance around the room, 'that it might not be a bad thing for the country. Many of the Queen's disgruntled statesmen – and her subjects – would agree with them.'

Once upon a time, Faro would have disagreed strongly. His Royal Highness had a reputation for wildness and the frequent scandals surrounding him were suppressed with difficulty and great expense. Only marriage to an excellent virtuous Princess had tamed him.

He was very popular in Deeside and the indiscretions that many of his nobles had condemned would, when he was King, be dismissed light-heartedly.

'A dam' fine fellow, just sowing his wild oats, y'know,' is what they would all say. His past was one many a less illustrious elder son and heir to a noble house would emulate, as the natural thing to do.

'I see by your expression that you don't understand what all the fuss is about,' said McIntosh. 'But we have good reason to believe that there's a sinister motive behind this group who are using the Prince as a front. And once they have him on the throne, then they'll twist him around their little fingers. By fair means or foul,' he added slowly.

When Faro gave him a hard look he nodded grimly, 'You get my drift.'

'Blackmail?'

'The same. They'll soon make it obvious that they are in real terms far from being passionate patriots. The opposite in fact. What they stand to gain is that they will use their power to take over the country. And between us, His Royal Highness has left evidence of indiscretions, letters and so forth, enough to merit a national scandal if they were made public.'

'This is incredible. Whatever he did in the past, we're

66

talking about matricide, sir. It's well known that he doesn't get on with his mother. But matricide . . . '

'It's been done before – Medicis, Borgias.'

'That was in the Middle Ages, we're living in civilised times.'

'Are we? I wonder. Before you get virtuous about it, the Prince, we are informed, has no idea that they plan to get rid of his mother. He would not unnaturally be glad to inherit, but irritation with a parent is a long way from killing them off. If that was the way of it then most of us would be orphans. Nationally, there was never a better time for the Prince's Party,' McIntosh ended gloomily.

'In fact,' he added in a treasonable whisper, 'I doubt sometimes whether she would even be missed. The country as you well know if you read your newspapers is very anti-monarchy just now. They take badly to her pre-occupation with Balmoral. And, dare I say it, with John Brown.'

Faro had met the Prince of Wales and was relieved to hear that he was not personally involved in this treasonable plot. Apart from a high-spirited reputation for being both susceptible and unreliable where a pretty face was involved, Faro found him witty, roguish and intelligent. He didn't doubt that Bertie would make an admirable and responsible king some day.

'The plan, if plan there is, is being presented to the Prince by a body of his admirers, earnest well-wishers and loyal Englishmen.'

'And Englishwomen perhaps?' Faro added. He could see it was just possible that the Prince might be manipulated by the ambitions of one of his current aristocratic mistresses.

'You have a point there, Faro. The theme is that the country is being mismanaged under the present Government by a monarch who has so little interest in her subjects, she hardly ever deigns to appear in public. She prefers to hide away most of the year with her wild clansmen in the Highlands of Scotland.

'And to many Englishmen anything north of the Tweed

means that the people still live in caves. The only interest most of the wealthy have is in buying land, estate and titles. They don't see the real country.'

It was true. In ever increasing numbers they came up twice or sometimes only once per year to shoot over their vast estates, have a continuous house party for several weeks and then disappear back to the Home Counties. These were, in fact, the notorious absentee landlords whose advent spelt ruin and desolation to the Highlands of Scotland.

McIntosh drained his glass. 'And, of course, you must see the drift of this plan. If they succeed and the Queen is got rid of then the Prince will inevitably be full of terrible remorse. Worse than that, he will only ever be a puppet king. They will make sure of that. They will make the laws, he will sign the State documents but one step out of line and they will need only to whisper one word in his ear.'

'What do you want me to do, sir?'

'Word is that the Queen must be in London for the State Opening of Parliament next Monday.'

'But that's less than a week away.'

'Exactly.' McIntosh counted up on his fingers. 'We can expect her to leave here on Friday or Saturday at the latest. So you have four days to find the killer before he strikes.'

'But that's impossible—'

'Nothing's impossible, Faro,' said McIntosh sternly. 'Use your much vaunted powers of observation and deduction on this. We're putting you on extended leave. You stay here until the Queen is safely back at Buckingham Palace. Understand?'

Rubbing his chin thoughtfully, he added, 'The fewer people who know you're here the better.'

Realising Bella's talent for gossip, not to mention Tibbie and the eagle eyes of all the locals, Faro said vaguely, 'I expect it may have got around that my visit is purely social. For my aunt's ninetieth birthday.'

'Keep it at that, if you can. I understand Purdie's a top man at Scotland Yard. Normally this would have been a case for the Aberdeen police. Fact is with the murdered girl having been a servant at Balmoral, etc., etc. It's all in the letter I had from the Chief Constable. Take Purdie into your confidence, Faro. In the unlikely event that he doesn't know all about this already.

'Get his help,' he added desperately. 'Don't be too proud to ask. Between the two of you, you should be able to thwart this attempt. Get John Brown on to it too. He's loyal and devoted, by all accounts. You've met him, of course.'

'The day I arrived—'

Reluctantly Faro told the Superintendent about the Queen's dogs, but the reaction he had dreaded wasn't forthcoming. McIntosh merely dismissed it as somewhat eccentric behaviour to be expected of a Royal personage.

'Whatever next, Faro?' he said brusquely. 'But do not be side-tracked. This other matter is vital. Prevent the murder, Faro, without trampling on too many Royal toes, or outraging too many duchesses.'

'That won't be easy, sir.'

'Use your influence with Brown, indulge him about the dogs. Enveigle yourself into the Castle as much as you can. Look around. You're sharp-eyed. Good heavens, man, I don't have to spell it out to you.'

He paused. 'Incidentally, it's well known that the Prince hates Brown.'

'So does his brother Prince Alfred. The Queen was furious when he once refused to shake hands with a commoner, a mere ghillie,' said Faro.

McIntosh shrugged. 'Possibly that would go for most of the Royal children. In their eyes Brown is a peasant with an overblown idea of his own importance. Moorcock turned peacock is the Royal whisper. Have you heard the latest?' Without waiting for Faro's reply, he went on, 'He's now extended his power over the Queen by

69

introducing her to seances. Seances and spiritualists, if you please. Putting her in touch with Prince Albert.'

'I wonder who was behind that piece of inspired skulduggery.'

'Indeed. And who do you think goes into a trance and speaks in the Prince's voice, calling her "Liebchen" and giving her tips on how to rule the country?'

'Not Brown surely.'

McIntosh nodded. 'The same.' He looked at Faro curiously. 'What's the chap like? I mean, to exert all this influence over Her Majesty?'

'Sound as a bell, I'd say, loyal to the soles of his brogues. I hope you're not going to imply that he's involved.'

McIntosh smiled into his beard. 'Not at all, Faro. That never crossed my mind. It was something quite different I had in mind. Er – do you think, I mean . . . ' His eyes roved the room, searching for the right words to phrase that burning question, 'Is there any truth in the rumour?'

'What rumour?' said Faro innocently, deciding not to spare the Superintendent.

'Dammit, man, you know perfectly well. That he and Her Majesty are, er, well – to put it delicately – infatuated?'

Faro laughed. 'Don't tell me you are being influenced by the popular press, sir. She needs a strong man, another Prince Consort, a father figure, but that's all. Someone with all the trappings of pomp and self-interest stripped away. Someone who would die for her if necessary but is much happier to live for her.'

'I thought her Prime Minister performed that function,' said McIntosh, clearly disappointed. 'How does Mr Gladstone take all this adulation of Brown, I wonder?'

'You must realise from your perusal of the newspapers, sir, that she cannot stand the man. He treats her with awe and reverence. She was overheard and quoted as saying, "He treats me like a public meeting."' Faro shook his head. 'No, she needs a friend, not a lover. Someone she can be a woman with, let her hair down, take a dram, for heaven's sake.'

With a sigh, McIntosh picked up his gloves, smoothed them with his large hands and looked wistfully in the direction of his empty glass. 'And that is damned fine stuff.'

'It is indeed. Made at our local distillery up the road. A little more, perhaps?'

'Mm. Thank you. You were saying—'

'John Brown makes her feel like a woman, not a Queen Empress.'

'Rumour has it that he even chooses her wardrobe. Isn't that going a little far, don't you think?'

Faro smiled. 'Not at all. After all, this isn't the first time a Queen has been mesmerised by a commoner. Take Mary Queen of Scots and Bothwell—'

'Bothwell was an earl,' McIntosh exploded. 'Brown is a mere ignorant peasant. A ghillie, dammit.'

'A ghillie he may be but ignorant, no. He's a dominie's son, well read—'

'I suppose you're going to tell me this is a situation not unknown. Seems to arouse, er, um, passion in a woman of breeding, being wooed and won by a common soldier or servant . . . '

Faro glanced at the Superintendent and wondered what kind of literature he read in his spare time. 'On the subject of clothes,' he said hastily, 'Her Majesty has no interest in gowns. Hasn't had much since Prince Albert died. Tends to wear the same black satin in Edinburgh every year.'

'It has been noticed,' said McIntosh drily.

'I'm not a man fond of dressing up myself,' said Faro uncomfortably, 'but I insist upon being clean and tidy and I feel shabby black is hardly in keeping with the Royal image.'

McIntosh nodded. 'There's a story circulating that this Brown fellow was overheard saying to her, "Now what's this you've got on today, woman?" He didn't approve of what she was wearing.'

He guffawed. 'Apparently she listened to his criticism and meek as a lamb went back and changed into something more suitable. Can you credit that?' And slapping his thigh delightedly, he added, 'Man, it would be more than my life was worth to criticise Mrs McIntosh's gowns.'

Faro suppressed a smile, for the Superintendent's wife was known in the Central Office as 'The Tartar', managing to keep her large husband well and truly under her tiny thumb.

As Faro walked down the road to where McIntosh's carriage waited, the Superintendent said, 'Any chance of an invitation to lunch or dine at the Castle?'

'Not so far.'

'Pity. Couldn't you get Brown to arrange a meeting, talk about those dogs – lost, weren't they?' he added vaguely.

'Shot, sir. Dead.'

'Oh yes.' McIntosh was not an animal lover and obviously wondered what all the Royal fuss was about. 'Try to impress on Brown that Her Majesty owes you an audience. And it would be an excellent chance for a little quiet investigation.'

On the step, he turned once more. 'There's one question you haven't asked me, Faro.'

'And what is that, sir?'

'Who is the brains behind the Prince's Party?'

'I haven't the least idea.'

McIntosh laughed. 'You should, Faro. He's an old enemy of yours.'

'Really? I have accumulated a vast number of those through twenty years with the Edinburgh Police.'

'But not many as clever or as wily as this one.' And watching Faro's expression eagerly, he said, 'This time we think it is Lord Nob's handiwork.'

Lord Nob. Noblesse Oblige. A devil with a dozen

72

names and a dozen faces, whose background was noble perhaps, rumour had it, even Royal, but whose true identity no man had ever cracked and lived.

Their last encounter had been in what Faro's notes described as 'The Case of the Killing Cousins'.

On a stormy clifftop in Orkney he thought he had seen the last of his adversary. Faro groaned inwardly.

Closing the carriage door, McIntosh leaned out of the window.

'I see you recognise the gravity of the situation. This is one of national peril. This isn't something you handle alone, Faro. Get Purdie on to it, d'you hear,' he repeated. 'Believe me, you are going to need all the help you can get. We're relying on you, Faro. See to it.'

Chapter Six

Faro found Tibbie in the barn. She had taken under her slender wing the welfare of Steady. Loving animals great and small, she announced proudly that he had been given his dinner.

With the rest of the day to himself until visiting time at the hospital, the idea of sitting with his fishing rod by the banks of the Dee now appalled rather than appealed. Especially as he brooded upon the fact that every boulder might now conceal the hidden presence and watchful eyes of his old adversary.

Considerably more in keeping with his temper was the challenge presented by marching out to confront danger. And by solving the sinister mysteries looming around him perhaps he might finally outwit Noblesse Oblige.

Horseback was an excellent alternative to exploring the countryside on foot in search of clues. A rider could not only move faster, he could also penetrate less accessible areas than one in a pony-cart.

Steady seemed to agree with him and made no resistance to being saddled up. If it wasn't too idiotic, thought Faro, he appeared to be smiling knowingly. The cause, he discovered, was a slight malformation of the upper lip due to a couple of missing teeth.

As they trotted off down the lane, the pleasure of riding through a golden, crisp-aired day with the sun still at its zenith brought a delightful sense of well-being.

Ten years ago, before the advent of horse-drawn omnibuses in Edinburgh, this had been his usual method of travelling into the countryside on the track of criminals. But in town he never felt safe in the narrow crowded streets and wynds of the High Street and its environs. In that vast criminal underworld where lurked many hazards, a man on horseback was particularly vulnerable.

With a half-formed plan in mind he found himself drawn towards the area across the river where Morag Brodie's body had been found. He did not doubt the efficiency of Purdie and Craig and realised there was little hope of any overlooked clues – especially as he suspected the girl's body had been taken from the ruined mill on the Balmoral Estate, to be discovered on the road which, according to Purdie and his map, led to Bush Farm.

Was his obvious deduction the right answer? That this had been to divert suspicion to the discarded lover, Lachlan Brown?

Climbing the steep brae, with its twists and turns, he had an unexpected stroke of luck. The sound of creaking wheels and a farmhand emerged driving a haycart.

Faro drew Steady in to let him pass.

''Tis a fine day, mister.'

Faro replied in kind.

The man was middle-aged, cheery-faced. 'Ye've missed the Mains road, doctor.'

'Doctor?'

The man eyed the horse and Faro's tweed suit reflectively. 'Aye, sir, ye'll be visiting the maister. Een o' the bairns has the croup.'

Faro shook his head. 'Alas, I'm not the doctor, and I fear I'm lost.'

The man's curiosity was thoroughly aroused. 'Stranger to these parts, are ye, sir?'

'Not quite. I'm biding with my aunt Mistress MacVae at Easter Balmoral.'

The farmhand was immediately interested. 'That was an awfa' business about the fire—' Suddenly he pushed back his bonnet, scratched his brow. 'I ken who ye are, mister,' he added stabbing a finger in Faro's direction. 'I wasna' far out in thinking ye were the new doctor.'

'He is my stepson.'

'And ye must be Mistress Bella's nevvy, the policeman,' was the triumphant response.

'Correct.'

The man chortled delightedly. 'We've heard all about ye, sir. Solving all these mysteries.' And leaning forward confidentially, he added, 'Did ye ken that there was a murder hereabouts?'

'I did hear something of the kind,' said Faro vaguely.

'Aye, sir,' was the excited response, 'and what is more, I could show ye the exact spot, if ye'd care to see it.'

Leaping down from the cart, he led the way back and stopped by a bramble-filled ditch some twenty yards distant.

He touched the verge with his boot. 'Here, sir, this is where she lay. I'll no forget it in a hurry, sir. For it was me that found the puir lass,' he said proudly.

'You must be Jock?'

'The same, sir.'

This was indeed an unexpected piece of good fortune.

'Early morning it was, I was on the way up to the fields here. And there was this bundle of rags, I'm thinking. Then I saw it was a woman. Och, a drunken tinker, her hair was over her face. When I tried to wake her up,' he gulped at the memory, 'I thought it was mud dried on her dress. Then I saw it was dried blood. She had been stabbed in the chest.'

'Did you touch anything?'

'Nothing, sir. I ran and telt the maister. He's an invalid, puir body, been in a wheelchair for nigh on twa' years. He was right upset about it, told me to saddle up and ride into Ballater to get Sergeant Whyte. And Dr Elgin. There's been an inspector, a top man from London,' he added in tones of awe. 'He asked

76

me a powerful lot of questions – and the maister too. He has it all written down, just exactly like I've telt ye.'

Faro did not doubt that. 'Did you know the lass?'

'Everybody kenned Morag Brodie,' Jock said slowly. 'A foreigner, no' frae these parts, working up at the Castle. The Crathie Inn was een o' her haunts wi' the rest o' the servants.' Again confidentially he whispered, 'Aye, a fair bucket o' drink they took, but kept themselves to themselves, o'course,' he added with a wry smile. 'Superior to the rest o' us.'

He stopped to watch the distant figure of a woman, carrying a basket.

'That's ma missus. Brings ma piece to the end o' the road.'

The haycart trundled off down the lane. Five minutes later Faro emerged from the ditch without any new evidence but with an abundance of scratches from the close-packed bramble hedge.

At that moment he was thankful that this particular case was not his responsibility and that Purdie had the killer already in his sights.

Why then did it continue to trouble him? Was it the vague possibility that the murder of Morag Brodie had its origins in a plot to kill the Queen?

He sighed. His search for whoever killed the Queen's pet dogs seemed even more ludicrous in the light of Superintendent McIntosh's monstrous revelations.

From the distant hill, the echoes of gunfire, the faint plumes of smoke and clouds of birds rising indicated that the sportsmen were still busily engaged in the morning's activity.

Shading his eyes he stared across the river and wished he could see inside the mind of the assassin who at this moment lurked somewhere behind the granite walls of Balmoral Castle, tranquil in afternoon sunlight.

He turned Steady's head, briskly trotting downhill until they reached the river bank and the bridge which gave access to the Castle gates. As they entered the drive, a landau approached carrying four passengers.

Faro recognised General Ponsonby, the Queen's secretary, and Prime Minister Gladstone. Sitting opposite them were two large gentlemen. With only the most cursory observation, stolid countenances and military bearing betrayed them as the security guards, Captains Tweedie and Dumleigh.

The General, who knew him, bowed and obviously identified Faro for the others who now turned and regarded him intently.

As they disappeared he found himself close to the spot where the Queen's dogs had been killed. When his presence in the grounds was revealed to Her Majesty she would, he was certain, express her impatience if he did not have some substantial progress to report to Brown within the next day or two.

If word of the Queen's dissatisfaction with his investigations reached the popular press, then his whole reputation might be under threat. He could imagine Her Majesty's scornful reactions on her next visit to Edinburgh: 'Inspector Faro, you say. Have you no one else? Why, he could not even discover who killed our precious dogs.'

Suddenly aware that he was running out of time, he shuddered. He had at most four days to discover the dog-slayer and avert a plot to murder their Royal mistress.

This was Tuesday. At the end of the week the Queen left once again for London.

If she was still alive.

As he rode towards the Castle, the drive appeared to be deserted and he realised how easy it was to gain access to the Castle. No guards, no policemen. Just as the Queen wished it to appear, a normal country house.

Dear God, that it was so.

He looked up at the windows, all empty, close-curtained in tartan. He turned away, frustrated, helpless to avert the catastrophe taking shape within those walls.

As he started back down the drive the sound of loud barking presaged the appearance of three liveried white-wigged footmen, leading a selection of assorted dogs.

At the sight of his horse the dogs became even more agitated, while Steady greeted the tirade with remarkable calm, snorting a little but remaining aloof.

The footmen meanwhile with great difficulty and much disentanglement of chains at last succeeded in quieting their charges.

While Faro expected to be challenged on his right to be riding about on Royal property, they merely regarded him sullenly. Touching his whip to his hat in brief salute, he trotted past and out on to the road leading to the bridge, suddenly elated by the encounter.

Did the footmen normally walk the dogs? If so, had this been one of the duties of Lessing, Morag Brodie's drowned lover?

He was to find the answer to that sooner than he expected when, a few hours later, with Steady again saddled to the pony-cart, he set off once more for the hospital.

Bella greeted him cheerfully: 'I'm being let home tomorrow for ma birthday—' The door opened to admit a somewhat breathless Vince. 'I was just telling him the grand news—'

'You go on one condition, Great-aunt,' said Vince sternly. 'That you promise to take care and not do too much.' And turning to Faro, he added, 'Dr Elgin has given me the evening off. I wonder, could we have supper together? I'm told the food is excellent at the inn.'

'No need for that, lad. Tibbie'll give ye both a bite to eat.'

'That's all very fine, dear. But we're not going to impose on Tibbie. Besides it's time I made the acquaintance of the locals. Agreed, Stepfather?'

'Agreed.'

'Forgive me carrying him off, Great-aunt. He will be all yours, I promise, from tomorrow morning.' And to Faro, 'Ten minutes, at the entrance?' And turning back to Bella, 'I'll look in and see you two ladies later.'

In the next bed Nessie remained motionless, apart from her heavy breathing.

Bella looked towards her anxiously. 'The puir soul. She gets that upset, cries a lot about Morag. And the Queen's sewing. Always was a worrier, ye ken. The nurse had to give her something to make her sleep. Puir Nessie, she's upset at me going. She wants home too.'

'But where will she go?'

'She can bide with me, of course,' said Bella indignantly. 'No one goes without a roof over their heads hereabouts, Jeremy. There's always good neighbours. And cottages falling vacant on the estate. The Queen's a kind caring body, never forgetting them as has served her.'

She smiled at him, picking up a ball of wool and needles from the bed. 'Now off you go and have yer supper, lad. I have the heel of my sock to turn and then it'll be bedtime. See and come early for me in the morning.' He hugged her fondly, promising to do so.

Vince was awaiting him in the lobby and greeted the pony-cart with delight. 'No more walking today, thank heaven. It's not a very big hospital, but the corridors seem uncommon long. Especially as I have to attend both men and women patients and when Prince Albert designed the dratted building, he omitted to make any communicating door between the two wings. I cannot imagine how it hasn't killed Dr Elgin years ago.'

The coaching inn was busy, obviously extremely popular with locals and visitors alike. They found a corner table near a cheerful log fire and over an excellent meal of broth, roast beef and Athol brose, Faro told his stepson of his conversation with Purdie and the two policemen, and his meeting with Jock at the murder scene.

McIntosh's secret visit and the plot to kill the Queen, he left until the end.

Vince whistled. 'This is incredible, Stepfather. What a hornet's nest you've stumbled on this time. But you know, I'd wager that Inspector Purdie knows about it. And that's the real reason for his presence here.'

'My thoughts exactly. And the sooner we put our two heads together the happier I'll be.'

'Three heads, Stepfather, if you please. Don't forget about me. I want a part of this too.' Vince sighed. 'You've realised of course that time isn't on your side!'

'In this game, Vince lad, it never is,' said Faro grimly, glancing at his watch. 'Talking of which, since it's now past ten o'clock I had better make a move in the direction of the bar if we want to be served with any more drams.'

Pushing his way through the crowd, trying to claim the attention of the harassed barman, he was greeted by another customer, similarly employed.

'We have met before, sir.' At Faro's puzzled smile, the man laughed. 'You fail to recognise me without the wig.'

'The wig? Ah, one of the footmen—'

'Correct. I apologise for the dogs' unruly behaviour this morning. Horses can get very uppity.'

'Not at all.' And as both men received their order, Faro said, 'Perhaps you would care to join us. At the table over there.'

'Thank you, I have already eaten. I had arranged to meet some friends.' And looking around, 'I don't see them anywhere. I've just arrived and at this hour it is impossible to find a seat,' he added, following Faro through the crowd.

The footman had an English accent, and on closer acquaintance he was not so young as Faro had first thought. Perhaps about his own age, touching forty, with a pale rather melancholy face and quite startlingly pale eyes.

Holding out his hand he said, 'Peter Noble's the name.'

'Mr Faro. Dr Laurie.' Faro's warning glance in his stepson's direction established his wish to remain incognito.

'This is our favourite haunt,' said Peter, settling himself comfortably and lighting a cigar. 'Can't tell you what a relief it is to be warm for a change and to escape all those restrictions at the Castle. Oh, I beg pardon, do have one, gentlemen.'

Vince who had not acquired the smoking habit declined. Faro would have preferred his old pipe but felt it would be churlish to refuse and the chance of an excellent cigar rarely came his way. A moment later he was glad of his decision, appreciating a high-quality Havana obviously in keeping with the Royal household.

'Her Majesty is a regular tartar about this sort of thing,' Peter continued, puffing happily. 'Can't abide smokers or the tobacco habit. I don't think I'll be telling tales out of school for it's fairly common knowledge. The strict rule is all cigars and pipes are banished to the smoking-room. Even illustrious guests are so treated. And that isn't the worst. By Her Majesty's order, that particular door is locked promptly at midnight.'

He laughed. 'It breeds a camaraderie among the guests and servants, I assure you. A kind of conspiracy which does add a furtive enjoyment to their illicit activity. Some have been overheard saying it beats being back at Eton or Harrow. Especially as smoking is forbidden even in the privacy of their own rooms.'

The waiter approached and Peter accepted the large dram that Faro had ordered. He drank it gratefully and as Faro and Vince made their excuses, saying that the hour was late, and prepared to leave, Noble stood up and bowed.

'I do thank you both for your hospitality. Your table by the fire was well chosen. Indeed, I am most reluctant to leave, but I should go and join my friends.'

Faro observed that the footman swayed somewhat as

he added, 'Shall I tell you something, Mr Faro?' And without awaiting a reply, 'You can't imagine how deuced uncomfortable the Castle is. Even in summer, if summer ever exists in this Northern clime, for there are no fires then in the guest rooms. The windows admit draughts and I am told that getting into bed is like drowning in ice cold sheets. Her Majesty regards such niceties as warmth as a loosening of the moral fibre.'

He looked from one to the other. 'That's how it is for the guests. I leave it to your imaginations, gentlemen, what it is like for us poor underlings.'

At the door, Faro offered him a lift back to the Castle.

'I'm obliged to you, sir, but as a group of us come down regularly we take a hired carriage.'

As they waited politely for his friends to assemble, Faro wondered how he could get around to the question poised most urgently in his mind.

'Do you usually walk the dogs?'

'No, sir. But we are one short. I'm the newest arrival, so I inherit that lowly task. Last chap unfortunately got himself drowned.' He grimaced.

'Fellow called Lessing, wasn't it?'

'The same.' Peter looked at him curiously and Faro was saved any further comment by shouts from the darkness.

'Yes, over here. I'm coming.'

And with profuse thanks he ran a somewhat zig-zag course towards the carriage where his arrival was greeted with shouts of encouragement and urgency.

When Faro returned to the hospital next morning with the pony-trap in readiness to take his aunt home, Vince was nowhere to be seen. A pretty nurse told him: 'Dr Laurie is with a patient just now—'

'It's all right, nurse, I can find my way.'

In the ward he found Bella in tears. Putting his arms around her he wished her many happy returns of her birthday.

'It'll no be that, lad. No' without Nessie.'

Faro looked at Nessie's empty bed.

'Where is she?'

At his words she broke into noisy sobs.

'Oh, Jeremy, lad. It's awful, awful. I canna' believe it.'

'Why, what's happened? Where is she?'

'Dead. Dead. Last night. And her so well. I just canna' believe it. And it all happened while I was here, in the next bed. And her not a day over seventy, so strong and well until yon fire—'

Faro put a hand on her arm. 'Auntie, people do die from delayed shock. Vince will tell you that,' he added as his stepson appeared around the door.

'This is a bad business, Stepfather. So unexpected. Heart failure.' Vince looked puzzled as he turned to Bella. 'It's been a shock for you, but you'll feel much better once you're in your own home again. I'll look in and see you later. Promise now, not to overdo things. Take care.'

'I will that. But oh, I'll miss Nessie. We've been close friends for thirty years or more.'

As Faro put a comforting arm around her shoulders, she patted his hand. 'The Good Lord be thanked I have you at such a time.'

Over Bella's head, Vince nodded to Faro. 'I'm attending to a patient. We'll leave you to get dressed, dear. Do you need any help?'

'I can manage fine, lad.'

Outside the ward, Vince led him out of earshot to the nurse who was going off duty.

'Thank you for waiting, Nurse Roberts. If you would be so good as to tell my stepfather about Mistress Brodie's visitor last night.'

'Inspector Purdie, you mean, doctor? He came after visiting time and said he had to see Mistress Brodie urgently. He had a message for her from Balmoral.' She smiled. 'Some delicacies from the Queen for her old servant.'

'What kind of delicacies?'

The nurse frowned. 'He was carrying a box, tied with ribbon. Sweeties, I expect.'

'You would, of course, recognise the Inspector again? He might come by – er, to see me,' Vince ended lamely.

The nurse looked puzzled. 'We–ell, I didn't get a very good look at him. It was dark and, as you know, doctor, the hospital is strict about lamps at night when most of the patients are asleep. Lamps and candles can be dangerous unattended, if sick patients try to get out of bed—'

'Of course, of course,' said Vince.

Faro smiled. 'As a matter of interest, what does the Inspector look like?'

The nurse thought for a moment. 'Tall, clean-shaven. Seemed to feel the cold. Wore his muffler and greatcoat collar high.' She paused indicating her chin. 'And he kept on his hat.'

Vince exchanged a significant glance with his stepfather who asked, 'What time was this?'

'About nine o'clock, sir. We had just completed the evening rounds.'

'Where were you during this visit?'

'At the table there.' She pointed to the far end of the ward.

'You were present all the time?'

'Not every minute,' Nurse Roberts admitted reluctantly. She was beginning to sound exasperated at his questions. 'I mean, Inspector. Someone sent by Her Majesty personally. It seemed, well, most impertinent, especially when he had requested a screen for privacy.'

'A screen? Isn't that somewhat unusual? Do you normally provide screens for visitors?'

'If it is specially requested, we do. You know, husbands and wives, we like to give them a little privacy. Especially if there is someone sharing the ward.'

Seeing his look she continued hastily, 'Nothing improper, I assure you, Inspector. The screen was Dr

Elgin's idea but although the patient is hidden from the inquisitive eyes of the other patients, they are clearly visible to the staff,' she added sternly.

'How long were you absent from the ward?'

'Five – ten minutes. I had things to check in the linen room and when I came back he had gone. I went to remove the screen immediately. I was very quiet as I presumed in the dim light that Mistress Brodie was asleep. It wasn't until I made my last round at midnight that I discovered she was dead.'

She darted a helpless look at Vince. 'It could have happened any time, whether I was there on duty or not. Her heart gave out, doctor.'

'Of course, nurse. No one is blaming you,' said Vince.

'Before you go, what happened to the box of sweeties?' Faro asked.

'It was empty. We threw it away when we cleared out her locker.'

'Just one thing more. Had you met Inspector Purdie before?'

'No. Never. This was his first visit.'

'How do you know?'

'Well, he asked me to give him directions.'

'Thank you, nurse. You have been very helpful,' said Vince. 'See if Mistress MacVae is ready to leave, if you please.'

Watching her walk towards the ward, Vince said, 'Of one thing we can be quite certain, Stepfather. Nessie's visitor was someone impersonating Inspector Purdie.'

'And taking a great chance that the real Inspector Purdie wasn't known to the night-nurse,' said Faro. 'I would very much like to examine that empty box of sweeties.'

'Too late. It would have gone into the incinerator this morning with all the other hospital rubbish.'

Faro swore and Vince continued, 'Look, I was with Dr Elgin when he examined Nessie's body. There was nothing to indicate it wasn't natural causes.'

'But we both know how easily heart failure can be induced in a frail old woman. Stoppage of breath could be achieved by putting a pillow over her face.'

'But why? What on earth had she done to deserve being murdered?'

'It was not what she had done but what she knew.'

At Vince's puzzled shake of the head, he continued, 'I would swear that this has something to do with the murder of Morag Brodie. And I'd be prepared to wager a hundred golden guineas that the reason for Morag's murder is that she knew about the Balmoral plot and talked too much. Bella told us that Nessie had raved on about the Queen being in danger.'

Faro swore again. 'We should have been prepared for something like this. They had already tried to kill her by burning down the cottage.'

'They?'

'Oh yes, Vince. We are well out of the realms of the crime passionnel now. We are into political assassination.'

Vince's eyes widened in horror. 'You mean—'

'I mean the Prince's Party. I'd stake my life on it. And we have to find our bogus Inspector and quickly. Because his next victim is the Queen. And this time, we have to battle against the clock. He has to play his cards quickly.'

John Brown had confirmed that the Queen had to return to London for various State occasions. The first and most important, as McIntosh had said, was the State Opening of Parliament on Monday next.

'She doesna' give much notice,' Brown had grumbled. 'Often tells the servants, "We leave tomorrow." Then it's all hell let loose.'

Faro took his aunt home and her conversation rolled over his head as he reviewed the rapid turnover of events since his arrival. And he no longer doubted that another fragment of the puzzle, the slaying of the Queen's dogs, fitted neatly into his conclusions.

Chapter Seven

Bella was speedily settled in her favourite armchair, among birthday tributes including an Orkney shawl from Faro's mother and lace mittens from his daughters, Rose and Emily. The shawl was to be pinned with an amethyst and pearl brooch from himself and Vince.

But the occasion which had been so eagerly anticipated was marred by Nessie Brodie's death. Bella could speak of nothing else and the now tearful Tibbie added her lamentations at their neighbour's untimely end.

'Tell Tibbie about Nessie's last visitor,' Faro said, curious to hear the story in Bella's own words, and managing to get in a word between the sobs and exclamations of the two women.

'That Inspector, you mean. Nessie knew him well. He bided with them one summer when he was a wee lad. They were talking and joking together. Quiet-like but I heard every word. At least most of it,' she said apologetically. "How's your poor hand, Davie lad?" was the first thing she asked him—'

Faro suppressed a smile. Bella's excellent faculties did not include sharp ears. She was growing increasingly deaf but hated to have it noticed. He concluded she would make a poor witness as she continued:

'Of course, I didn't want to seem nosey especially when I saw that screen being put up between us,' she added huffily. 'So I pretended to be asleep—'

She was interrupted by a new arrival. Tibbie had opened the door to Inspector Purdie.

'Care to accompany us to Bush Farm, Faro?'

On the doorstep Faro made a point of introducing the newcomer to his aunt.

'You are Inspector Purdie?'

'I am,' was the cheerful reply.

Bella's baffled expression held a multitude of eager questions and as they walked down the path Faro glanced back over his shoulder. She was watching them intently, standing very still, a hand shading her eyes against the light.

Her reaction put the stamp of certainty on Faro's suspicion that she had never seen the Inspector before.

In the carriage, Purdie said, 'Craig has gone on ahead.' Smiling, he added, 'Glad you got your aunt home safely, Faro. A remarkable old lady. Which reminds me, I must go in and see Mistress Brodie at the proper visiting hour this evening.'

So he hadn't heard.

'I take it you didn't go in last night.'

'Last night? I'm afraid not. Craig and I went into Braemar for dinner which became rather an extended affair. And I don't like breaking rules, Faro, even hospital rules. Or wielding my authority unnecessarily,' he added sternly, 'unless it's life and death. And interviewing a woman whose house has burned down hardly fits into that category.'

'In this case it's a pity you were so conscientious. You might have saved her life.'

'Saved her life? What on earth do you mean, Faro?'

'I mean that she's dead.'

'Oh dear, how very unfortunate. But in the circumstances, I suppose we mustn't be too surprised. She was old and had sustained a considerable shock.'

'I rather suspect that she was murdered.'

'Murdered?' Purdie whistled. 'By what means?'

'Smothered most likely, if the box of sweets her visitor brought wasn't poisoned.'

'Faro, you astonish me.' Purdie looked at him as if he

had taken leave of his senses. 'Do you realise what you're saying? Are you sure of your facts?'

And without waiting for an explanation, he continued, 'I hardly need to tell you that one has to be careful in our profession not to regard every sudden death as suspicious. After all, what reason would anyone have for murdering a harmless old woman?'

'That we have still to find out,' said Faro grimly.

'Then I presume you have good grounds for your suspicions.'

'I do indeed. She had a visitor last night. Someone pretending to be you.'

'Me—?'

Faro cut short Purdie's angry protests. 'Hear me out, if you please. Since our bogus inspector took the trouble to have screens put around the bed, I suspect either poisoned sweetmeats or a soft pillow was the method used to hasten the cause of death certified by Dr Elgin as heart failure.'

'Good Lord. This is dreadful, dreadful. And I don't much care for someone impersonating me. What was he like?'

Purdie listened grimly to the description as recounted by the hospital nurse. At the end he sat back and sighed deeply. 'We've got to find him, Faro. I have a personal stake in this one. What makes it worse is that I knew the old lady. Stayed with her once. She wouldn't remember me, of course, it's more than thirty years ago. And I've changed a bit since then,' he added wryly.

'On the contrary, she remembered you well. She talked to my aunt about you. She was very proud of your distinguished career.'

Purdie sighed. 'How extraordinary.' He looked out towards the hills. 'My family farmed here a couple of generations ago. What amazing memories these country folks do have.' He sighed. 'We had better get Craig to start the usual procedures.'

'No. In this case, I think not.'

'But that's highly irregular, if you suspect murder.'

'What I want is to prevent another murder,' said Faro.

'How so?'

'By alerting our man that we're on to him.'

'Go on.'

'My theory is that if Nessie Brodie was murdered then it is because she knew something dangerous about her niece Morag's associates at Balmoral.'

As the carriage climbed the steep hill leading to Bush Farm, Purdie considered the landscape thoughtfully. 'Our visit here is not unrelated to the case then. We have almost all the evidence necessary to make an arrest once the Queen has left Balmoral.'

'Why wait until then?'

Purdie shrugged. 'Because I have been so instructed. The Prime Minister's instigation, I gather, that I am to keep as much as possible from the Queen.' And turning to Faro, 'Your guess is, I am sure, as good as mine as to who killed the girl.'

'I never guess in such matters. Matters of life and death, I prefer to be certainties, sir. Matters of conviction, supplemented by foolproof evidence.'

Purdie laughed. 'Come, come Faro. You can do better than that. Even the most rudimentary training in police procedure must have taught you that the first place you look for your murderer is in the victim's family circle. Who has something to gain? Who hated her, etc., etc.?'

'Precisely. But in this case there wasn't much to be gained in the monetary way. She had no family but her Aunt Nessie—'

'And I don't think by any stretch of imagination could that dear kind soul, God rest her, be a suspect.'

Purdie's expression was suddenly bleak. 'So where else do we look, Faro? Who have we left? There are not many contestants and Morag Brodie was known to have rejected Lachlan for James Lessing, a footman at the Castle, who subsequently drowned in a tragic accident.

Logically then, our suspects are down to one,' he added grimly.

'But Lachlan did save her from drowning—'

Purdie held up his hand. 'I know your argument, Faro. Why save her just to murder her? I think we have worked that one out. He saves her, believing gratitude will restore her love for him. But she refuses him. He goes berserk.'

Pausing he regarded Faro's doubtful expression. 'For heaven's sake, this is the standard crime passionnel. Happens all the time. You of all people should know that.'

'Let us say I have some reservations about the nature of the killing. In my experience, one stab to the heart rarely indicates a frenzied attack.'

'Is that so?' Purdie sounded exasperated. 'From the evidence so far, I don't think there is the slightest doubt that Lachlan Brown is guilty. Everything so far points to him. But this case must be handled carefully. We are on delicate ground here, the lad being kin to John Brown, and John Brown close to the Queen.'

Faro thought cynically about those in authority trying to keep the facts of life and death from the Queen, desperate in their anxiety that her 'dear Paradise' should remain unsullied. On the other hand, he was not at all sure that Her Majesty's somewhat morbid preoccupation with death could not deal with a local murder. She might even relish it.

Opening the carriage door, Purdie regarded him intently. 'You get my drift, I think, without any further elaboration.'

Faro hesitated before replying. 'There is one further point, sir. My mysterious visitor whose carriage you observed yesterday was Superintendent McIntosh of the Edinburgh City Police.'

'I know the Superintendent—'

Faro finished his brief account of McIntosh's visit and

his fears for the Queen's safety with, 'He thought you should be told. If you don't know already.'

His searching glance of his companion's face told him the worst.

'I do know, Faro. And now that the cat is well and truly out of the bag, if you hadn't deduced it already, you will understand the real reason for Scotland Yard putting me on to this case. As I told you when we first met, your presence here was an almighty stroke of good fortune.

'And even before your disclosures regarding our old adversary Lord Nob, where you have the advantage over me, in a personal encounter, I was considering enlisting your help. Ah, here is Craig now,' he added, putting a finger to his lips. 'We will keep this information to ourselves, if you please.'

'If you are intent on making an arrest, you would have more chance of finding Lachlan at the Castle with Brown at this time of day.'

'Ah, we are ahead of you there, Faro,' said Purdie with a mysterious smile. 'At precisely this moment he should be on the hill with the Queen's picnic party. I thought we might seize the opportunity of his absence to search his cottage.'

Craig approached them, his face bright with triumph. He held up a knife, its long blade worn with constant use and sharpening, and in the horn handle a cairngorm stone.

'Here is your evidence, sir. Look what I've found.'

Purdie took it gingerly.

'That looks like blood to me, sir,' said Craig excitedly pointing to dark stains on the blade.

Purdie nodded, a little non-committally, thought Faro. 'Show us exactly where you found it.'

Craig led the way to a woodpile at the side of the bothy. 'It was hidden, sir. Down at the back. I nearly missed it.'

'May I?' Faro examined the knife briefly.

'What do you think, Faro?' asked Purdie.

'Surely you recognise the skean dhu, sir, the all-purpose knife every Highlander prides himself on wearing in his hose? I would suggest that its murderous appearance is perfectly in keeping with its normal function.'

'And that is?'

'It's used by ghillies for disembowelling deer, skinning rabbits and the like. In a society less preoccupied with etiquette it was used as table cutlery. To cut meat and the throats of its owner's enemies.'

'So this could be the murder weapon?' said Purdie eagerly.

'It could. Except that one would expect to find one identical in every Scots household from here to the Canadian Rockies and beyond.'

Craig was not to be outdone. 'But look at the stains, sir,' he insisted.

'I hate to disappoint you, but I suspect they are of animals' blood,' said Faro.

'Why should he hide it then?'

'I think it was less likely to have been hidden than accidentally mislaid.'

Craig looked mutinous, clearly disappointed. He turned to Purdie for support. 'What do you think, sir?'

'I think Inspector Faro may have a point. But there again, the knife might have been used for a more macabre task. So we must retain it as possible evidence, until we make further enquiries.'

And watching Craig rewrap the skean dhu in a piece of sacking, he continued, 'Well, Faro, are you still willing to accompany us?' And observing his reluctance, 'I would feel happier if you could overcome your scruples on this occasion. It may be of crucial importance to our enquiry.'

'Very well.' As they walked towards the bothy Faro asked, 'What else do you expect to find besides a knife that may or may not be the murder weapon?'

Purdie shrugged aside the question. 'When the Queen leaves Balmoral she sometimes takes with her members of her staff especially recommended. There is a rumour that Brown is anxious for the lad to go to London to continue his studies. A fact not without some significance.'

'Get him away from past indiscretions, is that what you mean?'

'And particularly the scene of the crime.'

'If he is guilty.'

'I am more inclined to "as" he is guilty, Faro. I shouldn't put too much credence on that word "if". You surely realise that we cannot risk a possible murderer leaving under cover of Her Majesty's entourage.'

'How do you propose to stop him?'

'Let's say we won't make it public. We will simply restrain him under lock and key until the Queen leaves.'

'What if John Brown protests? I can't imagine him taking that lightly.'

'John Brown or no John Brown, I shall formally charge Lachlan with the murder and have him escorted to prison in Aberdeen. Craig is ready to take care of such arrangements.'

Purdie smiled. 'Once Brown is convinced of Lachlan's guilt, he will accept the implications of allowing freedom to a murderer who, having got away with it once, might be considered excellent material for recruitment by some sinister organisation.'

'The Prince's Party, for example?'

'The same, not to put too fine a point on it.'

Perhaps Purdie was right, thought Faro. The game was too big and too dangerous to take chances.

Lachlan Brown's bothy stood in the annexe to the main farm building, a barn before its more recent conversion into a labourer's cottage.

As was the country custom, the door's only fastening was a latch. There would be little to search, two rooms where Faro expected the only evidence to be of a young bachelor's indifference to tidiness.

Instead, he was startled by the presence of a piano occupying a large portion of the living-room. Obviously it was not for show amid such simple white-washed walls. Music sheets of Schubert, Brahms and Bach indicated that it was in constant use.

The rest of the bothy was similarly surprising. Lachlan seemed to have exercised considerable care in choosing one or two small pieces which, like the piano, might be equally at home in Balmoral Castle.

The bookshelves displayed a variety of books which testified to Lachlan's taste in literature and suggested to Faro that their young owner deserved a better life than that of a Balmoral ghillie.

At his side Craig was examining the books curiously.

'See all this crime stuff, sir,' he said to Purdie.

'That our suspect is interested in reading about crimes doesn't mean that he also commits them.'

'But here – this is an axe murder case.'

'Craig, come away,' said Purdie patiently. 'I read such material regularly, as I am sure Inspector Faro does,' he added and when Faro smiled, he said, 'There now, be assured, Craig. It has given neither of us an overwhelming desire to murder anyone. Other than recalcitrant constables, that is. Now, come along.'

As Craig joined them in the bedroom, there were more surprises in store. A postered bed with a patchwork quilt took the place of the usual straw pallet; other refinements comprised a press for clothes, a wash-stand with toilet articles and an escritoire. On the white-washed walls, the paintings included a small Landseer.

Good taste abounded and, over all, a surprising air of opulence. Had this not been a farm bothy, its furnishings would not have shamed the lodging of a young man of quality.

One thing was becoming abundantly clear: John Brown's protégé was no simple village lad. And Faro stood by, ill at ease, suppressing a natural distaste for searching through even a murder suspect's personal possessions.

As Purdie and Craig showed more enthusiasm for the

task which they conducted with police thoroughness, he noticed with dismay that neither had been schooled in the same methods as himself. By Faro's rules, the search completed, all items should be carefully replaced to give an appearance of never having been disturbed.

Craig suddenly turned from the escritoire and said, 'What's this, now?'

He held up a thick wad of banknotes. Faro and Purdie watched him thumbing through them. 'Four hundred – five hundred pounds.'

'And where do you think he might have got such a sum?' Purdie said to Faro.

Craig whistled. 'A small fortune, sir.'

'A fortune it might be,' said Faro. 'But one I see little reason to link with Morag Brodie's murder. Unless—'

'Exactly, Faro,' said Purdie slowly, as Craig replaced the banknotes in the drawer. 'Unless. And I think we might conclude from this particular evidence that we're on the track of something much bigger than a rustic murder.'

And for once Faro had to agree with him.

As they were leaving the bothy, Purdie swore.

There was John Brown coming along the lane. He was alone and as he approached his greeting was tinged more with alarm than curiosity.

'Ye're wanting to see me?' he asked Purdie. Then he noticed Craig with the sackcloth bundle under his arm.

'Well, what's that ye've got there?'

Purdie disregarded his pointing finger and pretended to misunderstand the question. 'It is Lachlan we have business with.'

'What sort of business would that be?' Brown demanded suspiciously.

'When can we expect to find him at home?'

Brown shrugged. 'He's awa' visiting. Ballater way. That's all I can tell you.'

Purdie's usually bland face registered the dismay of a

97

hunter thwarted of his prey. 'When do you expect his return?'

'Late tonight. Mebbe not. I canna tell ye.' He grinned. 'The lad is mebbe courtin', ye ken. But I'll let him know ye called. Ye can depend on that.'

And touching his bonnet, he opened the gate, his eyes sliding anxiously towards the sackcloth bundle. Then to Faro he said, 'Have ye any information yet for Her Majesty?'

'I'm afraid not. These things take time.'

Brown's shrug was disbelieving. 'Her Majesty is getting gey anxious. She's wishful to have the criminal apprehended afore she leaves.'

Watching Brown's retreating figure, Craig said, 'Shall we go into Ballater, sir?'

'For what reason?'

'To apprehend Lachlan Brown, of course. I'm sure the proximity of a railway station has not escaped you, sir.'

'Come, come, Craig. You can do better than that. He would hardly disappear without taking his belongings. Or more important, his five hundred pounds.'

'But we have the knife.'

Purdie shook his head. 'We have, but he doesn't know that yet, does he?' And at Craig's anxious expression he went on, 'I don't think we need worry about him eluding us. He will be back. You can bank on it.'

On the way back to Crathie, Faro recounted to Purdie his quest for the Queen's dog-slayer and his suspicions that Morag Brodie had been murdered in the ruined mill and her body then transported over to Crathie.

Purdie looked very thoughtful and as Bella's cottage came in sight Faro rapidly added his account of his meeting with the dog-walking footmen and of his subsequent encounter with Peter Noble.

'Very interesting, very interesting indeed,' said Purdie. 'Especially that connection with Lessing. I think you might have stumbled on to something very significant indeed. And I must confess it does alarm me. I am more than ever certain there is not a moment to be lost.'

With a promise to meet later that day, they parted.

Inside the cottage, the tiny parlour was already crowded with well-wishers and neighbours.

Bella greeted him excitedly and gave the answer he had expected.

'Jeremy, that wasna' Inspector Purdie.'

'I assure you it was.'

'Then that wasna' the man who came in to see Nessie.' And shaking her head, she added firmly, 'He didna' look a bit like that.'

Chapter Eight

Faro was finishing his third cup of tea and resisting a profusion of pies, scones, bannocks and Dundee cake, made by Tibbie and the neighbours to mark the grand occasion of Bella's birthday and welcome home.

Loosening the two lower buttons of his waistcoat he realised that he was out of practice in the marathon eating stakes. A week of this particular good life and he would be unable to get into his clothes, and as the latch was raised heralding a fresh influx of well-wishers into the already overflowing parlour, he decided on retreat.

Looking down over the stairhead, he saw the new arrival was Lachlan Brown. Greeting Bella he handed her a delicate china figurine which also looked as if it might have had its origins in Balmoral Castle.

'It has a tiny hair crack – here,' he said apologetically at Bella's pleasurable exclamations. 'I'm afraid the Queen threw it out—'

'Oh, laddie, laddie. It's lovely. Ye're that kind.' She hugged him delightedly.

'It is no better than you deserve. We're all glad to have you back with us, Mistress MacVae.'

'Ye'll have some tea. Or a dram.'

Faro hovered indecisively, watched him carry cup and plate towards the door. A moment later Tibbie climbed the stairs.

'So that's where ye are, Jeremy. Lachlan wants a wee chat wi' ye. He's in the garden,' she added concealing her curiosity with utmost difficulty.

He found Lachlan on the wooden seat, staring out across the hill, looking if possible even more sullen and remote than he had at their first meeting.

Turning round he made no attempt to shake hands. 'I'll not beat about the bush, Inspector. I am here only because Johnnie insisted that I should see you. It's about Morag Brodie,' he said abruptly. 'I didn't kill her, whatever they are trying to prove. Yes, sit down, if you please.'

Faro regarded him narrowly. Black-haired, white-skinned, the lad was handsome enough on a good day to turn any lass's head; rebellious, with an arrogance that stemmed, Faro suspected, from being kin to the Queen's favourite.

'The point is, can you prove your innocence?'

Lachlan shrugged. 'She said she loved me. Then she met this other fellow. I don't see why they think that gave me good reason for murdering her.'

Suddenly the rain that had been threatening since morning began. Lachlan gave an exasperated gesture towards the drops that fell around them, heavy as coins. 'Is there somewhere we can talk?'

'Of course.' Faro led the way indoors to his room.

Lachlan sat down on the edge of the bed, considered his clasped hands. 'I did not kill Morag,' he repeated dully. 'I happened to be passing by when the accident happened. I jumped in and saved her – or haven't they told you that?' Without waiting for Faro's reply, he said, 'As soon as I got her on to the bank, I dived in again and tried to get Lessing. But I was too late.'

Lachlan sighed. 'Even if I had hated Lessing – and I didn't – I wouldn't stand by and watch any man drown.'

Faro was almost inclined to believe him, bearing in mind the surprising character of the bothy. From his vast experience of violent men, Lachlan Brown seemed too finely drawn and sensitive to have stabbed Morag Brodie in a blind and brutal fit of jealousy. Especially as the lad might have had the pick of a much wider range of elegant young ladies than the servants' hall at Balmoral could offer.

Suddenly he was curious to hear more of his background.

As if interpreting his thoughts Lachlan said, 'All right, Inspector. You had better have the truth. I expect it will come out sooner or later. I was only marrying Morag because she was having a child.'

So Bella had surmised, thought Faro, as Lachlan continued, 'Oh, it wasn't mine. But I was being paid handsomely for my trouble, a pension of two hundred and fifty pounds per year to give her child a name.'

Two hundred and fifty pounds a year was five pounds a week. The salary of an upper servant at Balmoral was the same, which might also mean that if Lachlan lived carefully he could exist in comfort for the rest of his life.

'And who was this generous benefactor?' Faro interrupted.

'Ah, that is a question I cannot answer.'

'Cannot or will not?' asked Faro softly.

Lachlan smiled. 'No, not from any delicacy or discretion. Just because I don't know either. The offer came from "A Well-Wisher" on Balmoral notepaper.'

'You have the letter in your possession?' asked Faro eagerly.

'Not even that. I was told to destroy it and that the bank in Ballater had been given instructions.'

'You were not in any doubt? You did not think that, for instance, it might be a hoax?'

'Not after I checked with the bank and found it correct in every detail.'

'Every detail. Such as?'

'There were no terms. Merely the payment. The first deposit of two hundred and fifty pounds had been made in good faith.'

It all sounded a little cold-blooded and hinted that

whoever was responsible for Morag's pregnancy was a man of wealth and importance. As for Lachlan, he was taking this somewhat murky business remarkably well. He was either innocent or he was a very glib liar.

'All that was required of me was that I declared Morag Brodie as my wife "by habit and repute" before two witnesses in the Scots fashion.'

'A marriage that would never stand up in a court of law outside Scotland.'

'Exactly, Inspector, but it would preserve her respectability. So what had I to fear?' said Lachlan cheerfully. 'Besides Morag left immediately to return to her duties at the Castle. There was no consummation, the marriage was to be kept secret until the Queen left for London.' He shook his head. 'I never saw her again and I did not feel inclined to bring up the matter when I was questioned by the police. Johnnie advised me to keep quiet.'

Faro could understand why, since this dubious undertaking gave Lachlan an even more valid purpose for getting rid of Morag Brodie while retaining her mysterious dowry. Murders were regularly committed for far less monetary gain.

Inspector Purdie, he was sure, would be very interested in this new piece of information.

'Johnnie disapproved strongly, but he agreed to be a witness. And Dave Grant. Their discretion can be relied on implicitly,' Lachlan added, 'although they both did their utmost to talk me out of it.'

'I am not surprised.'

'I did give it some thought, truly. But the marriage was to be in name only. There was no further obligation. The money was the main temptation. I have been supported by the Brown family all my life until now. Gives me the chance I have always wanted to study the pianoforte.' He smiled sadly. 'A dream was suddenly a possibility.'

'Did you never wonder why you were chosen for this rôle in Morag Brodie's life?'

Lachlan shrugged. 'I have no idea. She was pretty,

103

intelligent and I hope they get whoever killed her. I liked her well enough and I'm sorry she's dead. And not only because of the lost annuity.'

He laughed bitterly. 'Save your disapproval, Inspector. As a love child myself, abandoned by an unknown father, I realise that the state of idiocy known as being in love requires a measure of blindness. I prefer to keep my eyes wide open.'

His words brought to Faro echoes of his stepson's railings against his own illegitimacy – except that Vince's mother had been more fortunate in meeting Jeremy Faro.

'How old are you, Lachlan?'

'Twenty-two.'

Almost the same age as Vince, thought Faro, another parallel in two lives that were otherwise poles apart.

'Have you any family?'

Lachlan looked at him sharply, was about to speak and then looked out of the window. 'Uncle Johnnie is my family. All I have here. He isn't really my uncle, of course, although I should call him so. He is a kind of fourth cousin twice removed.'

His smile transformed his face with a shaft of familiarity. Where had he seen this lad before?

'How long have you lived here?'

'I was fostered by the Browns when I was still a small child. Orphaned, you know,' he added casually.

'Do you know anything about your parents?' Faro asked gently.

Lachlan's eyes shifted to the fireplace, his expression as bleak and implacable as its adornment of solemn china dogs.

'No.' And with a determined effort to change the subject, he added harshly, 'I had another reason for coming to see you, Inspector. I presume you were part of the police search of my home.'

'Reluctantly, yes. I don't approve—'

'Please don't apologise,' Lachlan cut short his excuses.

104

'I might have expected something of the sort. I have been told Inspector Purdie is very thorough and quite ruthless in his acquisition of evidence. I have nothing to conceal and I might have let it go at that but Johnnie insisted that I tell you. I had five hundred pounds in banknotes in a drawer in the escritoire.'

Faro remembered it being counted.

'There is forty pounds missing. Perhaps you can throw some small light on that mystery.'

'No. I can only say that I was present when Inspector Purdie and Sergeant Craig counted the notes and the sum of five hundred pounds was intact.'

Lachlan nodded. 'Nevertheless four banknotes are missing. In case you are curious, this has nothing whatever to do with my, er – marriage settlement. It represents money I was given, a gift, recently.'

'How recently?'

'Very recently,' said Lachlan firmly. 'A legacy. From a source I am not at liberty to disclose.'

'Has Mr Brown any theories on the money's disappearance?'

Lachlan hesitated a moment. 'He is as puzzled as I am.'

'Some passer-by—'

'No.' Again the voice was emphatic.

'But your door is left unlocked. Tinkers, for instance?'

Lachlan laughed. 'Inspector, our doors are never locked and while tinkers might remove – and frequently do remove – objects outside, which they regard as under the sky and therefore any man's fair game, they have scruples – no, fears or superstitions would be more appropriate – about house-breaking. A term of imprisonment locked behind bars is worse than death to them.

'Besides, there have been no tinkers in the neighbourhood since my last visit to Ballater—' Biting his lip, he cut off too late the betraying words.

Faro's mind was racing ahead. 'I would like to help you,' he said, 'but unless you are frank with me . . .'

'I can tell you no more. I have already told you more than I should.' Lachlan stood up. 'I see my visit has wasted your time. I am sorry—'

'Before you go. Do you know anything about a lost skean dhu?'

'A worn blade, horn handle with a cairngorm stone in the hilt?'

'The same.'

'Where did you find it?' Lachlan's eager delight made nonsense of this being the murder weapon.

'Sergeant Craig found it behind the woodpile.'

'So that's where it was. That is Johnnie's favourite dirk, given to him by Prince Albert. He lent it to me a couple of weeks ago when we were skinning rabbits. I mislaid it. Johnnie was very angry and we searched high and low. We did blame the tinkers. May I have it please?' he said putting out his hand.

'I'm afraid not. It has been taken away by Sergeant Craig. As evidence,' he added heavily.

'Evidence?' At Faro's silence, he laughed softly. 'Och yes, I see it fine. It would have its uses as a murder weapon. After all, that was its original purpose—'

They were interrupted by the arrival of Vince who threw open the door and announced that he had put all his patients to bed and was sorely in need of a dram.

Lachlan was disposed to be friendly to the newcomer. He talked about the best places to eat and the best places to fish. He was instantly transformed into a knowledgeable and enthusiastic countryman.

He left shortly afterwards, declining Faro's invitation to accompany them to the Crathie Inn where they were to dine, since Vince had little interest in the birthday party fare on offer. He would however accept a lift in the pony-cart as far as the Bush Farm road.

At their destination, Faro went over the day's events and the details of Lachlan's visit.

'He was right, Stepfather. Morag was pregnant, early stages. Dr Elgin told me. That Scots marriage though.'

106

Vince shook his head. 'Very cunningly thought out, don't you think? Could it be that the father was a member of the Royal entourage?'

Faro gave it some consideration. A well-known method of paying off discarded mistresses, the higher the lady's position on the social scale the more likely the gift would be accompanied by a title or an estate. But in the case of a maid at the Castle, the sum offered to some willing local lad would seem like a fortune.

'Known as the rich man's hasty exit from an embarrassing situation. I fancy that the Queen must be well aware of such matters.'

Vince laughed. 'Despite her pretence that servants do not exist below the waist and that the piano's limbs must be decently covered. You think Lachlan was speaking the truth about this mysterious benefactor?'

'I do. But I don't know why, lad.'

'I expect it has occurred to you that his reluctance to reveal the source of this money might well point to a more sinister connection with visits to Ballater.'

Faro nodded grimly. 'That Ballater might be the present headquarters of the Prince's Party. Is that what you mean?'

Vince nodded. 'And that Lachlan might be up to his ears in the plot. I think you should look very carefully into that young man's background, Stepfather, especially bearing in mind that he has just returned to Ballater after a long absence. A scholarship to Oxford, no less.'

'Really?'

'So Dr Elgin tells me. Can you beat that? What would a ghillie's lad be doing at Oxford? Why not St Andrews, or Edinburgh? Even I never aspired to Oxford.'

Faro suppressed a smile. Because I could never have afforded to send you there, he thought, even if the idea of an English university had entered my head. This was the 'lad o' pairts' with a vengeance.

Outside the cottage hospital, Vince said, 'I fancy Lachlan's absence would bear looking into, Stepfather, if it hasn't been done already.' Turning, he added, 'I don't suppose it has escaped your notice that his pale skin, so unusual in a country fellow, could be something else.'

'Prison pallor? Is that what you have in mind?'

'The same.'

Settling Steady for the night, Faro went into the darkened cottage. It was late and in due deference to Bella's great age and recent sojourn in hospital, the visitors had gone long since.

Creeping upstairs as quietly as he could, a board creaked under his foot and his aunt called out:

'Jeremy? I'm still awake.'

Turning up the lamp he saw she looked tired, but glowing and happy, like a small child at the end of an exciting birthday party. From underneath her pillow she handed him a silver cigar case.

'This was my dear man's. He would have wanted ye to have it. Been lying in a drawer for years. Tibbie came on it again when I was away, and she was cleaning. It was all tarnished.' She touched it lovingly. 'See what a bit of polish does. Vince told me ye smoke cigars sometimes. I want ye to have it while I'm still here and can see ye having the pleasure of it. Here, take it.'

Inside, under the Royal coat of arms, the inscription read: 'To Ben MacVae, a loyal servant. Albert.'

Thanking her with a hug and a kiss, he put the cigar case into his jacket pocket, resolving to fill it with fine Havanas at the earliest opportunity.

Faro's first visitor next morning was none other than the Prime Minister. An imposing figure with white hair and side-whiskers, Mr Gladstone bore an anxious expression which was either natural or induced by the gravity of his visit.

Ushered into the parlour by a curtseying Aunt Bella, Mr Gladstone accepted her offer of tea and bannocks.

'I would be delighted with a little refreshment. I have

been up since six this morning and have already walked ten miles. At a measured twelve minutes per mile,' he added proudly.

He dismissed Faro's remarks of appreciative amazement. 'I trust you will not take it amiss that I am calling upon you informally. John Brown has alerted me to your presence, sir. Your name is not unknown to me in connection with the visits to Edinburgh by Her Majesty the Queen—'

His momentary pause, eyes lowered, almost amounted to genuflection, thought Faro with some amusement.

'—and with security arrangements and dangers to her Royal person averted. All of which you have managed so skilfully to handle. Most skilfully and courageously,' he added in a whisper.

Did he always speak like this, in the manner of a Member addressing the House or reading a carefully prepared speech? And Faro suppressed a smile, remembering that the Queen's aversion to Mr Gladstone was because of his subservience.

'I come to you, sir, on this occasion as a supplicant.' Mr Gladstone placed his fingertips together as if about to deliver a sermon. 'A supplicant, sir. In direst need. For time is of the essence. Her Most Gracious Majesty the Queen' (again the lowering of eyes and voice), 'Her Most Gracious Majesty's life is once again in mortal peril. Mortal peril.'

Faro felt a quickening sense of disaster looming ahead. 'You have reliable information to that effect, sir?' he interrupted sharply.

'Only the merest hint, alas. A young man who was an – er, employed in the capacity of – er, surveillance of the Queen's safety. Very much undercover, you understand, sir. Very much. Discovered a threat to Her Majesty in none other than the Royal Household.'

Pausing dramatically, his hand upraised, he let the words sink in. 'Other attempts in the open have failed or have been frustrated. But this was daringly planned to take place by the Royal fireside. Such audacity. Breaking the sacred sanctity of hearth and home—'

'This man, Prime Minister—'

'I am not at liberty to discuss his identity. Except to say regretfully that he is no longer with us.'

'Paid off?'

'Dead,' said the Prime Minister hollowly. 'Pray do not question me further, Inspector.'

Could this be Lessing, the drowned footman, Faro wondered? If so, that threw a completely new equation into the plot. He would have loved to ask, but had no option but to respect the Prime Minister's wishes.

'Does your information concern an attempt at the Castle?'

'Indeed, sir. Have I not made that abundantly clear?' Mr Gladstone added indignantly.

'I had presumed so. And that this attempt must be imminent.'

'Imminent, indeed. As Her Majesty leaves Balmoral at the end of the week for the State Opening of Parliament, time is of the essence and we have very little—'

Too little to waste in verbiage, Faro thought in exasperation, wondering how any urgent business ever got through Parliament past its Prime Minister.

'You suspect this will come from within, that it is to be a domestic murder attempt?'

Mr Gladstone winced visibly at the word 'murder'.

'And from someone close to the Queen? One of the servants perhaps?'

'Servants, sir. I can hardly believe that one of Her Majesty's staff would commit blasphemy by touching the Royal person. Besides, all the staff are hand-picked, with excellent references. And those at Balmoral are particularly reliable. Most come from families who have served the Royal household since the Castle was built.'

Drawing himself up to his full height he regarded Faro disapprovingly. 'Loyal to a man, sir. They would

110

willingly lay down their lives for Her Gracious Majesty. As I would, sir. Willingly.'

Faro felt uncomfortably that these dramatics were rather overplayed. 'I should like to see records of these servants. I presume that their particulars are on file.'

'Indeed. There is a register of when each one took up his or her position, plus the salary and any information regarding special qualifications for the Royal service.'

'Is it possible that I might have access to this information?'

'Indeed, yes. If you think it will help. I shall have it put before you.'

'No, Prime Minister, that would not do at all. This inspection must be sub rosa. If it is seen that I am carrying out an investigation then we lose out by alerting the assassin.'

Again Mr Gladstone winced at the word. 'If you wish, sir, but I thought that the true purpose of your visit here was being kept secret. That officially you were merely on a visit to your aunt.'

'That is what I thought, and hoped, a week ago,' said Faro with a sigh. 'My aunt, alas, is a dear good soul but is not renowned for her discretion. She is inclined to talk about her family and their preoccupations at some length.'

Mr Gladstone's face fell. 'That is a pity. A great pity.'

'Indeed it is. I expect that every movement I make is under observation.'

'In that case perhaps you will accompany me. We might make it look as if we had met by accident while I was taking one of my walks.'

'No, Prime Minister. That will not do at all. I would opt for a discreet social visit. In the evening perhaps when there are fewer prying eyes. And with your permission, I shall bring my stepson Dr Laurie, so that it looks as if we have arrived merely for a game of cards.'

'Capital, capital,' crowed Mr Gladstone delightedly.

Then he added nervously, 'Do you play cards for money, by any chance, Inspector?'

'I would not dare, sir. There is an old adage about lucky at cards, unlucky in love. I seem to be lucky in neither, alas.'

The Prime Minister nodded eagerly. 'I have in my time tried to exert a little influence on His Royal Highness in the matter of gaming. At dinner at Abergeldie he invited me to play whist. I queried, "For love, sir?" To which he replied, "Well, shillings and half a crown on the rubber." Protocol demanded that I submitted, especially since the Prince's suggestion of such paltry stakes did show a nice point in manners.'

Faro was spared the search for a suitable response when Mr Gladstone continued, 'Perhaps I should bring to your attention that Sergeant Craig has inspected the servants' register recently in connection with the – er, unfortunate murder that Inspector Purdie of Scotland Yard is investigating.'

'The Inspector is aware of the Queen's danger.'

'Fully aware. But since he has not yet had the honour of protecting the Royal person, we consider that you have experience in the matter which might be invaluable to him. Especially as Her Gracious Majesty is acquainted with your methods.'

As Faro accompanied the Prime Minister to his carriage, he asked, 'What are Her Majesty's commitments outside the Castle before she leaves?'

'She plans a visit to Glen Muick tomorrow, a picnic followed by a salmon leistering later in the day. The fishermen attract the salmon to the surface by torchlight and spear them.'

Gladstone frowned suddenly as if the dangerous potential of that wild place at sunset had just occurred to him. 'Perhaps it would be advisable for you to accompany us. I shall arrange it.'

And leaning out of the carriage window, he added, 'I understand that you are carrying out a minor investigation

112

at Her Majesty's behest concerning the recent decease of two of the Royal dogs.'

Faro nodded glumly and the Prime Minister continued, 'May I presume that you are on the track of some clues?'

'Alas, no.'

'A pity. A pity indeed.'

Faro did not like to depress the Prime Minister further by telling him that the identity of the Queen's dog-slayer and the prospective assassin were undoubtedly one and the same.

Chapter Nine

Inspector Purdie arrived ten minutes after the Prime Minister had left. Aunt Bella, whose supplies of warm hospitality were inexhaustible, offered tea and bannocks.

'If you would be so kind as to butter them, not too thickly, Mistress MacVae.'

Congratulating her on her recovery, Purdie commiserated with her on the loss of her neighbour. This threatened to bring about floods of tears and Bella retreated hastily.

'I am sorry. I did not realise—'

'They have been friends for thirty years or more,' said Faro. 'Nessie was like one of the family.'

Purdie sighed. 'Apart from the burned-out shell of the croft down the road, how little the place has changed since my boyhood visit. I do not remember ever meeting you then,' he added regarding Faro curiously.

'I was in Orkney a good deal.'

'A pity our visits never coincided. Your aunt has a remarkable memory for faces and names.'

Faro laughed. 'So good one is never sure how much is memory and how much hearsay. The old are like that.'

'I have thought so too. The young have more important matters to concentrate on.'

Tibbie carried in the tray, Bella at her heels. She said, 'I'll leave you gentlemen to your tea. Perhaps you'll pour, Jeremy. That pot is difficult until you get to know it,' she added with a warning nod in his direction.

Faro did as he was bid and Purdie tackled the modest repast with vigour and enthusiasm.

As Faro finished his account of Lachlan's visit and his mention of the missing banknotes, Purdie showed no signs of surprise. 'They will be returned,' he said grimly. 'I have the matter in hand.'

'Craig?'

Purdie nodded. 'He confessed. Didn't know what came over him. He was needing money urgently, overspent on his next week's wages. Apparently the unfortunate fellow has got into debt. Not too precise about details, but when pressed he admitted to gambling for large stakes at the Crathie Inn.'

Faro swept his excuses aside. 'This amounts to stealing, Purdie. I need not stress to you that this is a particularly serious matter.'

'I agree and I have reprimanded him severely.' Purdie's tone was light but Faro was not convinced. For a police officer in search of evidence to appropriate banknotes or any other possessions was a matter for instant dismissal with Edinburgh City Police.

'I have great faith in the lad,' said Purdie. 'This is the first time he has succumbed. He was hoping that in a few days he could replace the money or send it back anonymously.'

And determined to close the subject he said firmly, 'Now to business. Did the Prime Minister's visit throw any more light on the Queen's danger?'

Faro decided not to mention his inspection of the register in case Purdie took it amiss. 'Did you know they had an undercover man who gave them the hint about the Prince's Party?'

Purdie nodded. 'Lessing, you mean?'

'So it was him.'

Purdie smiled. 'Naturally, Faro, he was sent by the Yard as soon as we realised there would be an attempt at Balmoral. I gather he found something out but had his unfortunate accident before he could be of any further use.'

'In the circumstances can we continue to dismiss his drowning as accidental? Especially as it also sheds some light on the murdered girl.'

Purdie helped himself to another bannock. 'Unfortunately we will never know now whether he was recruiting her or whether she merely knew more than was good for her and was apt to be indiscreet when she had taken drink.'

Faro considered for a moment. 'There is another possibility which I am sure has occurred to you.'

'And that is?'

'That Lessing did not drown after all. That he was swept down river and that someone was waiting for him.'

'You mean, they hit him on the head or stabbed him—'

And Faro found himself remembering the bloodstained skean dhu.

'—Then he was dumped in the mill race? Is that what you are saying?' Purdie shook his head. 'Far too much of a coincidence, don't you think, that the murderer should have anticipated the accident and have been waiting his opportunity downstream – at the exact moment?'

He dismissed Faro's theory with a shrug. 'No, Faro, I'm afraid that won't do at all. Let us not forget that the Prime Minister is inclined to exaggerate. I still maintain that Lessing drowned. However, you have succeeded in raising some uncertainties in my mind. In the circumstances a visit to the Castle would be well worthwhile.'

'Then you will be glad to hear that I have engineered an invitation to cards this evening. My stepson will accompany me and I have been promised an opportunity to scrutinise the servants' register. Perhaps you would care to join us.'

'Capital, Faro. As you know, I left that part of the investigation to Craig. As well as taking their statements. But now . . . ' His sigh emphasised Craig's unreliability.

As Purdie was leaving he thanked Bella graciously. She

116

watched him from the window while Tibbie gathered up the tray from the parlour.

Faro smiled. 'I don't get my bannocks buttered, Auntie,' he said teasingly. 'Nor am I allowed to eat without removing my gloves.'

'Ah, so you noticed did you?' said Bella.

'That he only ever takes off one glove seems curious. What is wrong with his right hand, anyway?'

Bella held up her hand dramatically with the two middle fingers covered. 'That's what happened. On that holiday he spent with Nessie. She never forgave herself although it happened away from her cottage. He was playing with a saw.'

She sighed. 'It was the first thing she asked him when he came to visit her that last night.' And when Faro looked puzzled, she went on, 'The man she thought was him. No wonder she said she would never have recognised him again. "How's your poor hand, Davie?" He said he had managed fine all these years. "You can get over anything, if you work at it." '

This explanation provided another answer for Faro as the two men set off in the pony-trap later that evening. The fact that Purdie could light a pipe and keep his gloves on and his pride intact. To overcome such a handicap as a policeman and reach the height of his profession was admirable indeed.

Vince had sent a message that he would be found at nine thirty in the Crathie Inn which put paid to his part as one of the card players. He would be disappointed at missing a visit to the Castle, thought Faro, as he and Purdie were received at the entrance.

A liveried footman led the way through a maze of carpeted and curtained corridors bedecked in the now familiar Balmoral tartan. Black, red and lavender on a grey background, it had been designed by Prince Albert himself.

The late Prince's influence was everywhere, from the

117

bust crowned in laurels to the permanent evidence of the Queen's melancholy veneration of widowhood. Death was the predominant theme. Their progress was over-looked by stags' heads gazing down at them in the last glass-eyed throes of mortal conflict while Mr Landseer's paintings depicted the dying agonies of stags and rabbits, and the bloody corpses of game birds.

The corridors were ill-lit too; Faro had imagined a more extravagant use of wax candles in a Royal residence. They followed the candelabra held high amid frequent warnings:

'Mind the steps, gentlemen, if you please. This is a bad one. Take care now.'

Such remarks suggested that there could be a succession of broken ankles for the unwary or the poor-sighted, conclusions echoed by Purdie's whispered, 'One needs sharp wits for the hazards of this journey.'

At last they were ushered into the Prime Minister's study where a fire of dismal proportions did little to enhance the pervading gloom of dark oak panelling, leather sofas and, for light relief, the soundlessly snarling tiger-skin rug.

The Queen's secretary Henry Ponsonby rose to greet them. Faro had met him before in Edinburgh and had great respect for the General, who combined efficiency with an admirable economy of the jargon of official-dom.

'Mr Gladstone is in audience. He sends his apologies for his absence.' He pointed to the desk. 'These are the registers you wish to inspect, gentlemen. I understand your concern is with newcomers, is that not so?'

'It is.'

Ponsonby opened the ledger, turned up the lamp. 'Then perhaps I might be able to save you some time. Most are footmen, casual employees taken on for service during the period of the Queen's residence. Such persons would have their credentials investigated thoroughly, of course.'

118

'And if they come from beyond Deeside?' Faro indicated two addresses in Perth.

'Then they would generally be recommended by other members of the Royal family, or other households. Such as Abergeldie, the Prince of Wales's residence.'

Faro exchanged a glance with Purdie. To build up a dossier on servants from far afield and find out whether they were who they pretended to be would take several days.

When he said so, General Ponsonby shook his head. 'The Queen either brings servants with her or in most cases employs tenants from the estate or Crathie. This is a small tight area, convenient on a temporary basis, so that they can return to their own homes when the Castle is closed. In some cases, you will observe, we are already into the second generation of servants from one family.'

He ran a finger down the list and ticked off various names: son of, daughter of. 'I can personally vouch for all of these.' Then raising his head he glanced across at Faro. 'You will have to look elsewhere for your criminal, sir.'

Faro was startled by his directness until he realised that Ponsonby presumed he was still engaged in the quest for whoever had killed the Queen's dogs.

'What about Abergeldie Castle?' asked Purdie.

'You mean the Prince of Wales's servants?' Ponsonby shook his head. 'That is the business of the Master of the Household. Besides, the Prince is not in residence and the Castle is empty meanwhile.'

At the door he turned. 'The Prime Minister informs me that you wish to be included in the Queen's outing to Glen Muick. That is so? Excellent. Pray be so good as to ring the bell on the desk when you wish to leave.'

The servants' register went back to the first Balmoral Castle. Many were retainers employed by Sir Robert Gordon who had then passed into Royal service with the new building and its illustrious owners.

'Excellent character, trustworthy and dependable' were the usual marginal comments.

'I think we can safely dismiss these worthy souls from among our suspects,' said Purdie.

The list of newcomers and temporary staff did not take long to compile:

'Morag Brodie, lower servant, recommended by Mistress Nessie Brodie, seamstress to Her Majesty. (Deceased)

'Lachlan Brown, ghillie, recommended by Mr John Brown.'

And 'recommended by H.R.H. Prince of Wales', four names:

'Peter Noble, footman.

'James Lessing, footman. (Deceased)

'Captain Horace Tweedie, security guard.

'Captain David Dumleigh, security guard.'

Purdie crossed out Lessing and Brodie and indicated the footmen:

'One dead, one to go. Or are we on the wrong track? Who would you consider the most likely, Faro?'

'Noble has access as footman and so has Lachlan Brown as ghillie.'

'I am inclined to add two more to my list,' said Purdie.

'The Captains?'

'Precisely. I consider anyone who has been in the Prince of Wales's service is worthy of careful attention and even now I am awaiting a full report from the Yard.'

Faro studied the list. 'If we learn that the two Captains are beyond reproach, then the only newcomers are Lessing and Noble.'

'And as Lessing is marked deceased, that leaves us with Noble.'

Purdie shook his head. 'You are forgetting Lachlan Brown. And there is one other whose name is not on our list.' He sighed heavily. 'But that I think I will keep to myself until my enquiries bear fruit.'

Faro thought of Craig. Had Purdie reasons of his own for suspecting his colleague? 'I trust your enquiries will not take too long. We have only three more days,' he warned.

'Two more, to be precise,' was the grim reply as Purdie rang the bell on the desk.

In the carriage, Faro decided that Purdie must be told about Lachlan's Scots marriage.

The Inspector was very impressed with this new information.

'Ah, Faro, at last, the perfect motive. Perhaps this is precisely what we needed.'

As they parted inside the Inn, he declined Faro's invitation to a dram. 'It has been a long day and I have various notes to make.'

Watching him climb the stairs to his room, Faro hoped that he would have a chance to become better acquainted with the Inspector. His usual experience was of detectives and policemen working closely on a case, their lives often depending upon one another, yet parting afterward each with only the faintest inkling of the others' personal lives.

In the bar Vince had just finished supper. Thrusting aside his plate with a sigh of satisfaction he said, 'I fancy I shall be eating here regularly. Hospital food.' He grimaced. 'Reminds me too much of medical school. I do miss good cooking. Having been thoroughly spoiled by our Mrs Brook, I was expecting more of the same from Great-aunt.'

And accepting the dram Faro set before him, he asked, 'Now, what news?'

Faro outlined the events of the day, his visits from Lachlan and from Mr Gladstone, ending with the visit to the Castle. Considering the list, Vince said:

'I wonder about the footman drowned in the Dee. By the way, I wandered down to the kirkyard, saw his grave and Morag Brodie's. Thought it might inspire me with some splendid deduction and enlightenment. It didn't.

121

Only to consider how ironic that the girl who was with him had survived only a few days, to be murdered. And that John Brown would not take kindly to his lad being under suspicion of murder.'

'Indeed, no. How would he be able to face the Queen again? Betrayal from within—'

'What are you hinting at? You surely don't think John Brown—'

Faro laughed. 'Heavens no. Brown in a plot to kill the Queen? That is beyond belief. Especially as Bertie has no love for his mother's favourite servant. Can you see the Prince's Party approaching him with such a proposition?'

'Not by any stretch of imagination.'

Then Faro remembered wryly that it was usually those who were beyond his stepson's stretch of imagination who had proved to be guilty in past cases.

'Do I detect you have a certain reluctance to consider Lachlan's guilt, Stepfather? Two hundred and fifty pounds per year to go through a form of marriage valid only in Scotland smells fishy to me. And that five hundred pounds could have been the pay-off from the Prince's Party for getting rid of the girl and Lessing. Surely Lachlan's presence at the drowning episode is highly significant? I am suggesting that he might well have engineered the whole incident, Stepfather.'

He paused, then with a disappointed shrug, said, 'You don't look very convinced.'

'I'm not. Not certain sure as I would wish to be. As I have to be on my own cases when I am in at the beginning and have viewed the bodies myself and studied their relation to the scene of the crime. There are raw edges here that nag. My instincts tell me that there is some vital factor missing.'

'At least we can rely on Inspector Purdie,' said Vince.

'True. But he was not here when it happened either. I have the strongest feeling that the motives are all too obvious and that far from apprehending the murderer, the Inspector is merely at the entrance to the labyrinth. At present I am convinced of only one thing.'

'And that is?'

'Morag Brodie's murder is linked, somehow, with an attempt to be made on the Queen's life. And we have only two days left, lad. Two days to avert a national catastrophe.'

As they parted, Vince announced that Dr Elgin, knowing that Faro's short stay in Easter Balmoral was drawing to an end, had freed him from duties until midday, after the early morning ward round.

'I was thinking we might take a drive up to Bush Farm,' said Faro collecting him at eight. Steady trotted along happily through roads dappled with sunlight. The hint of autumn touching the treetops with gold was dazzling in its perfection and difficult to reconcile with thoughts of sudden violent death.

As they reached Bush Farm, John Brown was emerging from the gate. Flustered and bleary-eyed, he was in that condition the Queen was pleased to call 'bashful'. More accurately, he was still suffering from the effects of a heavy night's drinking.

Rumour had it that the Queen quite often participated in such an activity and could match him dram for dram. But no one really believed that.

'Lachlan?' he said in answer to Faro's question. 'He's awa'.'

Vince's look of alarm indicated that Lachlan, guilty, might have taken flight.

'Away where?' asked Faro politely.

'Away courtin' – mebbe. I dinna ken,' Brown grumbled.

'Courting?'

'Aye, that's what I said. I dinna ken where. That's a man's business and I dinna question him. If he wants me to know, then he'll tell me.'

'Mr Brown,' said Faro. 'This information might be vital.'

At Brown's suspicious stare, he hesitated only a

moment and then plunged on. 'The Queen's safety may be at risk.'

Brown looked astonished. 'Ye're no implying—'

'What I'm implying is that the Queen, and your lad Lachlan, may be in danger.'

Vince's admiring glance in his stepfather's direction said plain as words: Well, that's one way of convincing Brown to tell all.

John Brown shook his head vigorously in a valiant effort to gather together his thoughts. 'I dinna believe ye. No one would touch the Queen here. It's havers, man, havers.'

His laugh though scornful was not quite convincing. 'As for the laddie, he's awa' into Ballater. There's a lady he's acquainted with.'

'You've met her?'

'Once. She stayed a night at the farm here. Two-three years ago.'

'She isn't from this area?'

'She is not. A foreigner.' Brown sniffed disdainfully.

A coarser-grained fellow would have spat, thought Faro as he asked, 'You mean French or something?'

'Not at all. She's from up north somewhere. Doesna' speak the Gaelic at all.'

That covered a wide range of Scottish folk from the Borders to John O'Groats.

'She wouldna' be my choice for the laddie,' Brown admitted reluctantly. 'She's a wee bit older than himself. But then, an older lady is often verra attractive, even irresistible.' His expression softened as he looked across the river in the direction of the Castle and Faro remembered that the Queen also fitted the category of the older, 'irresistible' lady.

'May we take you down the road?'

'No. The carter passes this way in an hour or two. I'll no' delay you any longer.'

As Steady gained the main road with his two passengers, Faro urged him into a trot: 'I hope we're in time.'

'Time for what?'

'For Lachlan Brown.' Faro looked grim. 'I've been putting together a few observations and deductions. Remember the veiled lady we met when we arrived in Ballater.'

Vince's face looked blank.

'Of course, you were too busy with the scenery. But now I am having some second thoughts and indeed, I would not be surprised to find that she, and not Lachlan, is our quarry.'

'The source of the five hundred pounds he lied about.'

'Exactly. On the same theme, I am surmising that it was she he met the other night.'

'Wait a minute, Stepfather. Are you hinting that she might be working for the Prince's Party? And the hired assassin?'

'Perhaps even that. If our quarry is Lord Nob, then he frequently works with a woman accomplice. And I am quite confident that nothing about our mysterious lady will surprise me in the least.'

But in that, as so often was the case, Detective Inspector Faro was to be proved wrong.

As the pony-trap trotted briskly into the station, the train from Aberdeen had been signalled.

Their destination was the waiting-room, which they found occupied by an old man reading his paper in one corner and by Lachlan sitting close to a woman swathed in veils.

He was holding her hand.

As Faro walked quickly in their direction, Lachlan and the woman stared up at him. She gave a little cry of alarm, poised for instant flight. She tried to dodge past him but Vince blocked her exit, standing firm between her and the station platform.

'No – no,' she cried.

Faro decided on the bold approach. 'Madam, before you board that train and before I take you and this young man into protective custody, I would beg you to reveal yourself.'

Still protesting she retreated behind Lachlan, gathering her veils closely about her face.

'Madam, have the goodness to remove your veils.'

'No, no.' Her voice was a faint whisper. 'I cannot.'

'Then, madam, you give me no alternative.' And stepping forward, Faro moved so quickly that she could not escape.

Lachlan struggled against Vince's restraining arms and the other solitary passenger opened his mouth to protest. Then considering the odds, he thought better of it, buried his face in his newspaper and tried to pretend they did not exist.

Pinioning the woman's wrists, Faro pulled aside the veil.

Words failed him utterly as he found himself staring into the last face in the world he had expected to see. The anguished and bewildered countenance of a woman well known and once well beloved.

It was the face of Inga St Ola from his homeland in Orkney.

Chapter Ten

'Inga! For God's sake. What are you doing here?'

'I can tell you what she is doing here. It's none of your damned business.' And Lachlan took a threatening step towards him.

'No, Lachlan, please. Please, dear. I know this – this man.'

'You do?' Lachlan stared from one to the other.

'We are old friends.' Inga smiled thinly. 'From Orkney days.'

'Then we must tell him.'

'No.'

'We must. This has gone too far, Mama.'

'Mama?' Faro's voice was a whisper.

'Yes, Inspector. Lachlan is my son.'

Faro heard Vince's sharp intake of breath.

'He is my very well kept secret.' Inga continued to gaze at Lachlan fondly, squeezing his hand. 'I left him here more than twenty years ago . . . '

As Faro listened he was coldly aware of two things, Vince's heavy gaze and a sudden sickness in the pit of his stomach. In a great tide it threatened to overwhelm him, and in so doing, banished all other emotions, including the Queen's mortal danger and the possibility of lurking assassins.

Was it – could it be – that Lachlan was his own son? His and Inga's?

Taking the boy's hand again, she was saying proudly, 'Lachlan is one of my youthful indiscretions.'

127

'My father died before they could be married. A riding accident,' said Lachlan in defence of his mother's honour. 'Isn't that so . . . ?'

Again Faro found himself watching their lips move but hearing no sound beyond the tumult of his own heart. Aware of Vince very still at his side, he flinched before his stepson's stare that, his guilty conscience told him, reviled and accused him.

Vince also shared the brand of bastardy. But at least there seemed to be no resemblance between them except in their unfortunate circumstances.

He turned his attention again to Lachlan, regarding him harshly, unable to see even a fleeting likeness to the face that he shaved before the bedroom mirror each morning.

But now he recognised that the black hair, blue eyes and white skin he had thought of as typical of the Celtic Highlander, Lachlan had inherited from Inga St Ola.

Whoever was Lachlan's father, he was no adopted child. He was Inga's flesh and blood. And Faro was astonished that he had been so blind, and that the familiarity taunting him since their first meeting had failed to bring Inga to mind.

Suddenly he longed to get her alone, ask her some vital, searching questions. Vaguely he heard the guard's whistle, the train's engine. How could he stop the pair boarding the Aberdeen train?

But that was not their purpose. Inga walked towards the guard's van where a large package had been unloaded.

She regarded it sadly. 'This was to have been my wedding gift. At least it will still be useful in your kitchen.' And tucking her arm into Lachlan's, she laid her cheek against his shoulder with a sigh.

Faro could think of nothing to say, and regarding the boy's stony face, mumbled, 'A tragedy indeed.'

Had Lachlan allowed Inga to believe this was a love match? And the revelation that Inga St Ola was his

128

mother did not declare him innocent of murder. Much as Faro desired it should, it changed nothing.

Faro knew he must not, could not allow any influx of personal feelings to influence his judgement. But the enormity of his discovery was too terrible to contemplate.

He knew now that the prime suspect for Morag Brodie's murder might well be his own son. But what right had he to expect a son's love, should Lachlan learn that his father had not been killed in a riding accident but was Detective Inspector Faro who had deserted his mother and Orkney to serve with Edinburgh City Police?

He shuddered with distaste. The revelation that he might have a son was bitter indeed. The detective's son who was a murderer, involved in a conspiracy to assassinate the Queen of Great Britain. The publicity would not go down well at the Central Office. It would spell the end of his career.

But Lachlan was a stranger to him, his name assumed.

No one need ever know the truth, a small voice whispered.

But Faro would. And he wasn't sure that he could live with that knowledge for the rest of his life. He was bitterly ashamed of his cowardice.

He might see his son tried for murder, found guilty and hanged by the neck until he was dead.

A cold shaft of premonition seized him. Had he always suspected that a child might be the reason for his mother Mary Faro's report that Inga had suddenly disappeared for several months after their brief love affair and his departure to Edinburgh?

It had always been a possibility, resting dangerously in the recesses of his mind. Now, after more than twenty years, had it come home to roost?

'Let us take some refreshment before we return.'

He blessed Vince for thus taking the situation in hand. And for gallantly leading the way ahead with Lachlan, who after one swift frowning glance at his mother, followed.

He was grateful to have Inga on her own, although she displayed a sudden reluctance for his company. As she seemed anxious and determined to keep up with the two young men, Faro put a hand on her arm.

'Stay, Inga. Talk to me, for God's sake. Talk to me.'

'What about, Jeremy? What would you like to hear? The weather I left in Orkney? This year's crops?'

'No, dammit. Other times and things. We are old friends. When did we last meet?'

'Only last summer,' she said sharply. 'No need to make it sound like the last century.'

He made a despairing gesture, able to think of nothing but the question mark hanging above Inga's son, Lachlan.

'So what is the weather like in Orkney just now?' he said with a weak attempt at humour.

Inga gave an exasperated exclamation, regarded him angrily. 'Just like it is here, Jeremy. You know that perfectly well.'

Her sweeping gesture encompassed the sleeping mountains with their burdens of sheep and boulders. 'Just like this,' she repeated, 'without the trees.'

'I didn't mean that—'

She laughed shortly. 'I know you didn't.'

'Are you really in mourning? Or is that part of the rôle you are playing, Mrs – what-is-it?'

She stopped in her tracks, stared at him defiantly. 'Saul died three weeks ago. Or has that news not reached you yet?'

Saul Hoy was the blacksmith at Balfray Island, to whom Inga had been housekeeper and more than that, she once confided, for many years.

'I've been away from Edinburgh. I am truly sorry. How did it happen?'

'He'd been ill for some time. I found him sitting in the kitchen in his chair one morning.' Her eyes filled with sudden tears.

'I'm sorry, Inga,' he repeated.

Slightly mollified, she sighed. 'I shall miss him.'

'What will you do now?'

She shrugged. 'That was my main reason for coming to Scotland. Lachlan and I have always been close. He was always begging me to come to Deeside. Saul left me comfortably well off so now I may be able to purchase a house for us.'

'A moment, Inga. Did you by any chance give him money? Five hundred pounds to be exact?'

'Yes, I did. Saul left it to him. But I don't see—'

Faro groaned. 'No, you couldn't. Please go on.'

'Ever since Saul first took ill and we both knew it was final, we discussed what might happen. Saul, bless his heart, worried so about me. He urged me to think about coming here to Lachlan. The wedding came as a complete surprise—'

'Saul knew about Lachlan?'

She smiled slowly. 'Oh yes. He was the only person in the world I trusted with my secret.'

Faro stopped in his tracks. 'Inga. Tell me. I have to know – is Lachlan – is he—'

She smiled up at him defiantly. 'Go on. Finish it.'

She wasn't going to spare him and Faro took a deep breath. 'Is he my son?'

Again she smiled. 'And if he is, Jeremy Faro, what then? What will you do about it?'

'I will marry you, of course,' he said sternly.

Inga doubled up with laughter. So sudden, so shrill was her laugh that Vince and Lachlan halted, looked back, hesitated, until Faro signalled them to proceed.

'Jeremy Faro,' she gasped, 'you'll be the death of me. Really you will. You'll marry me, indeed. What about me? Am I not to be considered? What if I don't want to marry you?'

'But—'

'But nothing. I've lived very comfortably without you for more than twenty years, thank you very much.'

'Had I known . . . ' And Faro remembered his youthful flight from Orkney. Longing to be free, his ambition had made him luke-warm in his proposal that Inga might come with him. He had added, 'Eventually, when I am properly settled.'

Instead, she had passed out of his life and he had met Lizzie, with her young son Vince. And he had married her.

'To propose marriage to legitimise a child is, I consider, almost the greatest insult you could offer.'

So she had not known the details of Lachlan's Scots marriage?

Overwhelmed, confused, reduced again to stammering boyhood, all he could say was, 'I didn't mean—'

'I realise you didn't mean to be insulting. You thought you were being kind. And proper. Edinburgh manners have got through to you, Jeremy Faro,' she added bitterly.

Then suddenly she laughed again, laid an imploring hand on his arm. 'Let's not talk of it any more,' she said gently. 'It's past. Dead and buried with all the pain of long ago.'

They walked in silence the few yards towards the hotel Vince and Lachlan had indicated.

At the door, Faro said, 'I don't want to go in there yet. Come, let's walk round the square.' She made no resistance and he went on, 'You haven't answered my question yet, Inga.'

'Oh, I thought I had politely declined your proposal.'

Stopping, Faro seized her arm. 'Don't be evasive. Damn you, Inga. I want the truth. Is Lachlan my son?' And at her stubborn expression, 'I can count perfectly well, you know. I can ask him—'

'Don't you dare, Jeremy Faro. That would be unforgivable. How could you even consider such a thing?'

'That story about a father killed before he could marry you—'

'You have got it wrong, as usual. I was much more

imaginative than that. When he was young I told him I was friends with his mother who lived in Aberdeen. She died when he was born. I was with her at the time so I brought him here to grow up with the Brown family—'

'And he believed you?'

She shook her head. 'Not entirely. Not after we once stood by a mirror and looked at our reflections together. That told all. He was about fourteen. He gave a sob. Took me in his arms and said, "Mother, Mother. I've always known you were my mother. Why did you tell me you weren't? Do you think there was anything in this whole world I would not be able to forgive you?"'

She paused to wave to the two young men who had reached the hotel door and hovered indecisively.

'Coming,' Faro called.

'We were very close, Jeremy. Like you and your stepson.'

That was the moment when Faro guessed why Inga St Ola had never liked Vince when they had met in Orkney. It was quite understandable, for the love Faro lavished on his stepson could, by a single word, have been transferred to Lachlan.

As they made their way slowly across to the hotel, Faro said, 'Eating, at this moment, is an activity I can well do without. I hope you are hungry.'

'Oh, I am. Deeside gives me an enormous appetite. You can always take a dram and watch us eat,' she added mercilessly.

'Look. We must talk.'

But now, bleakly indifferent, she said, 'I don't see what else we have to say to one another. Really I don't.'

Watching the two young men with their hearty appetites and Inga not far behind them, Faro did his best to carry on a normal conversation.

It was not easy, especially with Vince's anxious 'What's wrong, Stepfather? Come, you must eat something. Is your stomach playing you up again?'

With his lack of appetite the centre of attention,

Faro snapped angrily, 'Oh do stop fussing. Keep your doctoring for the hospital, if you please.'

Vince's eyebrows went up a little. Eying his stepfather narrowly, he refilled Inga's wine glass. 'Very well, very well. Only asking, you know.'

Having been so ungracious, Faro insisted on paying the bill.

'Will you be all right?' Lachlan asked Inga anxiously. He had observed that she had been somewhat reckless in her consumption of wine. 'I am on duty shortly. The Queen's picnic.'

Faro took Inga's arm firmly. 'I shall see her safe back to her lodgings.' Then to Vince, 'Get Lachlan to drop you off at Beagmill.'

And without waiting for their reactions he led her to the railway station. There the small boy left holding Steady and the pony-cart was agreeably surprised by the unusually large coin pressed into his hand for these services.

Once aboard, Inga gave directions and said, 'Thank you, Jeremy. I'm grateful, truly. I just wish we could have met under happier circumstances.'

In answer to his question, she sighed. 'I have no idea how long I'll stay. Lachlan is going to need me now. This terrible business. I can't believe it. Murder? That's something that happens to other people, not to one's own family.'

'Did you know Morag?'

'I met her on my last visit. Before she got involved with this other fellow at the Castle. I found it unbelievable; she was so utterly besotted with Lachlan. And who could blame her?' she added with a proud smile. 'First love and all that.'

She laughed softly, leaning towards him so that her head almost touched his shoulder. 'We know how that can hurt, don't we, Jeremy? Everyone else sees the holes and crevasses, the yawning pit of disillusion, but we go on our happy blinkered way. Just like Steady here—'

134

'What did you think of the girl?'

'Very pretty, very flighty. A tease. But such a horrible end. And yet although I was shocked, when I thought about it, I found I was not completely surprised. Girls like that, who entice men, often end up disastrously.' With a shrug she added, 'And I do get instincts, feelings about people.'

She looked at him. 'You know how it is. The witch in me, Jeremy. It's still active. Something from that first instant of meeting. I often see very clearly. Like looking down a long lane, with an uninterrupted view.'

'"Look well upon the face of the stranger . . . "'

She nodded. 'Yes, Jeremy. You have it too, I realise that. Perhaps it accounts for your survival all these years in your dangerous job.'

'Tell me, what did you feel about her?' Could Inga contribute something vital that he had missed, never having met Morag Brodie?

'I seemed to see deep inside her, behind her eyes. She was not what she pretended. It was as if she played a part and sometimes hesitated, trying to remember her lines, as if the rôle she had chosen was too hard for her. I realised that she had tremendous vulnerability. That men would love her for it and would use her too. This extraordinary appeal, but she wasn't clever enough to handle it. In that instant I almost pitied her—'

She held out her hands. 'I wanted to gather her in. Warn her. And then I knew it was useless, whatever lay ahead I could do nothing to prevent it happening. It was already written,' she added heavily.

'And I made a resolve. If she was what Lachlan wanted, then I would do all in my power to help them. But I didn't think it would come to that. I also knew it was very one-sided. Lachlan was not enamoured. So when he wrote me that they had been married by habit and repute, I was taken aback. Hurt, too, that I had not been invited even as a witness.'

'Did he give you any reason for the haste?'

'I presumed the worst. That she was carrying his child. When I heard of the tragedy, of course, I came at once. I was shocked to learn that she had left him immediately after the marriage, such as it was, and that he had never seen her again.'

Faro wondered if she knew the full story, of the £250 and the mysterious benefactor, but she was asking the question he dreaded.

'I gather they have not found the murderer yet? Who do they suspect?'

Faro was saved an answer when she continued, smiling, 'I'm sorry, I suppose that is secret information. At least no one could suspect Lachlan, for which I must be thankful. And I gather he has been very helpful to the police.'

That was news, thought Faro cynically; obstructive would have been a better term.

On the outskirts of Ballater was a tiny private hotel, set among pretty gardens.

'This is where I leave you,' said Inga.

'When shall I see you again?'

Inga's face was in shadow. 'Do you really want to?'

'Of course I do.'

'Do you think that is wise?' A vestige of pain sounded in her voice this time.

He took her hand, held it tightly, not wanting to let her go. 'Wise or not, I would like to see you.'

'Very well. How about tea this afternoon?'

'Splendid,' he said, taken aback by her unexpected eagerness.

'Here, about four? Till then.' She smiled and he saw in the sudden dazzling radiance Lachlan's resemblance to her. Whatever Inga St Ola pretended, unless she had a twin sister, Lachlan was undeniably her flesh and blood.

And probably his.

Helping her down, wondering whether he ought to kiss her or not, he found the decision was spared him. Turning abruptly she hurried up the gravel path to the hotel door.

136

Watching her disappear inside, disappointed that she did not once look back, he climbed into the pony-cart.

His emotions in turmoil, he arrived back at the Crathie Inn. There his appointment with Inspector Purdie served to remind him that at four o'clock he could not take tea with Inga St Ola, for he would be on his way to Glen Muick and the Queen's picnic.

'Damn. And damn again,' he swore.

Chapter Eleven

The Inspector was comfortably ensconced at a table by the window. As they shared a dram, Faro recounted the morning's events, how he had met Lachlan's mother.

'An old acquaintance of mine from Orkney days.'

Purdie's eyebrows lifted in faint surprise, especially as Faro after a little embarrassed throat-clearing drank up hastily, in the manner of one eager to change the subject.

Purdie's bespectacled eyes glinted in amusement. 'So you are hinting that the money was honestly come by.'

'I believe so. Willed to the boy by her former employer.'

Purdie nodded. 'So we have settled that mystery. Good. Incidentally, I have returned personally to Bush Farm the banknotes Craig – er, removed. I shall recover it from him later,' he added grimly.

'How did you explain it?'

'I left the envelope on the kitchen table. I did not even try to explain.'

Faro frowned. 'Will that not leave young Brown with a poor impression of the police's integrity?'

'Transparent lies would be even less likely to impress him,' said Purdie. 'Besides I suspect that he is no stranger to fabrications. A Scots marriage, did you say? I have never heard such rubbish.'

'It happens to be true, sir.'

'It will never hold up in a court of law.'

'Except in Scotland,' Faro insisted, regarding him

138

thoughtfully. As so often happened, an English up-bringing had sadly blunted the Scots 'lad o' pairts' to the manners and customs of his ancient heritage.

'Hrmmph.' Purdie scowled. 'And what's all this salmon leistering the Queen is so interested in? Why doesn't she leave the catching of fish to her menials?'

'I presume it is all part of her wish to share in the peasant life of her tenants. She sees Balmoral as her own rustic Arcady.'

Purdie laughed harshly. 'Without any of the hardships. I am sure it has not gone unnoticed by you, Faro, that this is the sort of thing that brought Marie Antoinette to the guillotine. I, for one, will be heartily glad when I see Her Majesty safely aboard the Royal train in Ballater. This whole exercise has been an absolute farce, a waste of precious time, don't you think?'

And without waiting for a reply, he went on, 'It must be plain to our assassin by now that he cannot succeed when everyone except the Queen seems to know his intentions and is healthily alert. Don't you agree?'

Faro didn't. Through twenty years of dealing with violent criminals he had developed an acute sense of danger. 'I imagine there are always at least a dozen corners where an assassin might lurk unnoticed in the Castle. And another dozen weak spots in security ar-rangements, that have been overlooked by everyone concerned.' He paused. 'Except the assassin, of course – who must manage to stay one step ahead.'

'You are forgetting someone else.'

'Am I?'

'Yourself, Faro. We have it on record that in dealing with crime, it is Detective Inspector Faro who has always been that one step ahead.' He laughed. 'Why else did you think I wanted your help on this case?' And stroking his beard thoughtfully, 'Tell me, what is the secret of your success? Luck, care or intuition?'

Faro shrugged. 'A little of all three.'

'Let's hope for all our sakes that none of these attributes has deserted you. You are coming to Glen Muick?'

'I am. Perhaps you would care to share the pony-cart?'

'Thank you, no. I would offer you the carriage but I have various things to do, enquiries which may take some time.'

Purdie hesitated as if about to impart their nature, then shook his head, saying, 'I will see you there.'

Glen Muick was the Queen's favourite area. She loved its 'real severe Highland scenery', and the loch which could look noble or sinister according to the mood of the weather.

As Faro rode Steady along the narrow rough track by the loch, the glen whose name meant 'darkness' or 'sorrow' was living up to its name.

It could hardly have been less inviting. He had forgotten that visitors, expecting a deer forest to be a picturesque dense tree-covered expanse, found on closer acquaintance a sparse wood on the lower foothills and sides of burns. Above, the naked mountainside covered in huge boulders and wild heather stretched skywards.

He was thankful that his destination was not Alt-na-Guithasach, called somewhat inappropriately 'The Hut'. In the higher and more treacherous reaches of the mountain, the bothy had been built for the Queen and her beloved Prince Albert.

When he died it held too many memories for her to visit it. But she could not desert her dear loch, so seven years later she built the Glasalt Sheil by its shores, accessible by boat or road.

At last the house appeared against the distant hills. Across the heather the sound of guns reverberated. The afternoon shoot was still in progress.

Faro shaded his eyes against the light. Small puffs of smoke and birds rising into the sky indicated that the sportsmen had now reached the wilder stretches of the hillside.

140

Steady did not care for this distant activity. It made him nervous. In deference to his horse's distress, Faro decided to anchor the reins to a large boulder and strike out on foot across the heath towards 'The Widow's House'.

Keeping to windward so that he might circle the guns and approach by their rear meant hard going. He was no tracker and the gnarled burnt-out roots of heather clung to his ankles one moment, while the next he found himself slithering across a treacherous slope or ploughing through an oozing bog marsh.

Leaping across a tiny stream he missed his footing, tripped and fell headlong. The fall which winded him also saved his life.

As he hit the heather, the air above him whistled and he heard the unmistakable sound of a bullet slam against a boulder and ricochet into the water.

He raised his head timidly, expecting to see one of the Royal party hurtling towards him, angrily questioning his right to be there.

Preparing to give a good account of himself, he stood up and stared round indignantly.

There was no one in sight. He had the vast boulder-strewn landscape to himself but for a belt of stunted trees and a glacial rock of large proportions on the horizon.

Even as he considered that as the direction from which the gunfire had emanated, another shot rang out. Dropping like a stone into the heather, he lay still, no longer in any doubt that he was the target.

Around him all was silent as before and with a fast-beating heart, he considered his next move.

Suddenly he saw a movement, a head raised about twenty yards above him and hastily withdrawn. His assassin no doubt. And he cursed the fact of being unarmed and completely vulnerable to attack.

In a fist fight he was confident that he could hold his own, but he could do nothing against a man with a gun.

Except to escape by using guile and cunning.

The watcher had moved. Keeping out of sight, he heard

the footsteps of someone leaping through the heather,
They were heading in his direction.

He thought fast, realised he had one chance – only
one, and that was to lie perfectly still, play dead until
his attacker was upon him.

Keeping his head well down, he listened to the thump-
ing of his own heart. The footsteps were close now, he
could hear his assailant breathing.

He braced himself against another bullet thudding into
his flesh and when instead a hand touched his shoulder, he
sprang into life, with the speed of a coiled spring suddenly
released. In a second, the rôles were reversed. He had his
man, arms twisted behind him, face down in the heather,
cursing and threatening.

Turning him over, he discovered the startled countenance of Peter Noble looking up at him.

'Mr Faro. For God's sake, let me go. What the devil
has got into you? You're breaking my arms.'

Faro relaxed his grip enough to allow him to struggle
into a sitting position.

Noble stared at him ruefully. 'I thought you were
dead.'

'Then I am sorry to disappoint you.'

'Disappoint? What are you talking about, sir? I was
watching you come up the hill when someone back there
took a pot shot at me. At least I thought it was me. Then
I saw you fall.'

As Noble spoke Faro saw he carried no gun. He did
a quick calculation. If the footman had intended to kill
him out here on the hill, he would not have approached
empty-handed. In case his quarry was only wounded he
would have come prepared to make certain, to give him
the coup de grâce.

Noble looked round nervously, shaded his eyes against
the horizon. 'This really is too much.' And taking Faro's
arm, 'Hurry, sir. We're obviously in someone's line of
fire. They shouldn't be allowed, such rotten shots. No
regard for people's safety.'

Following Noble through the heather, Faro asked, 'What were you doing up here? Why weren't you with the guns?'

'I was sketching, sir.'

'Sketching in the middle of a shooting party?'

'I dabble, sir. Her Majesty is very encouraging. Come. I'll show you.'

He led the way up to the large rock, behind which were spread out his materials and easel. He pointed to the half-finished painting.

'It's a fine sheltered spot. As you see, quite safe from the guns. And a splendid view of Glasalt. At Her Majesty's request,' he added proudly.

'It's very good.' And it was. What was more, whether Noble lied or not the colour was still wet and to Faro's inexperienced eye, the composition represented several hours' work.

Noble's chosen site was also invisible from where he had been walking up the hill. On the road far below, Steady was happily cropping the grass where he had left him.

Now from over the hill another man appeared at the run. It was Purdie this time. Cupping his hands he was shouting, 'Faro – Faro.'

Faro came out from behind the boulder, waved vigorously.

Purdie stumbled over the heather breathing hard. 'I heard shots from this direction. There were no guns. I feared the worst.'

'I seem to have got myself in the wrong place.'

'You look a bit white about the gills.'

'Someone took a pot shot at Mr Faro, Inspector,' said Noble excitedly. 'Perhaps even two shots.'

Purdie's face as he looked at Noble registered disbelief. 'I was over at Glasalt.' He patted the telescope in his pocket. 'Keeping an eye on things. As I was scanning the terrain, I saw you leave the horse. I fancied you might be heading in the way of the guns so I sent Craig to direct you. Where is he, anyway?'

The three looked round. Of Craig there was no sign.

Ignoring Noble, Purdie took Faro's arm firmly, led him out of earshot. Staring across at the footman who was regarding his painting indecisively, he asked, 'Tell me, what exactly did happen?' He sounded worried.

'A bullet whizzed over my head, ricocheted. There was a second shot which, according to Noble, he thought was meant for him—'

'According to Noble,' repeated Purdie heavily.

'It could have been a mistake, sir. The Royal party are notorious bad shots—'

'Look again, Faro, see the direction the wind is blowing the smoke. There are no guns firing over this area.'

Again Purdie glanced back at Noble who seemed to have lost interest in the proceedings. Paint brush in hand, he was concentrating his efforts on Glasalt Sheil.

'There was no one else here, Faro. Except him.'

'True. But I didn't see any evidence of guns among his equipment.'

Purdie dismissed his theory about Noble's lack of a gun.

'He could have concealed it just a few steps away in the heather. If you were merely wounded, then he had only to snatch it up. God, man, you were unarmed.' And looking round, 'The heather is the perfect place for hiding spent bullets too.'

Purdie sighed. 'I think you are taking this far too lightly, Faro. I regard what has happened as a serious attempt on your life. All the evidence seems to point in that direction.'

'In the circumstances I'm afraid I have to agree with you, sir,' said Faro glumly.

'It's what I've been expecting. That we were to be the targets.'

'We, sir?'

Purdie smiled grimly. 'Indeed, yes. The second bullet wasn't for Noble. It was for me. I was in full view dashing across the heather towards you. I don't need to impress upon you the gravity of the situation, Faro. Our murderer is getting desperate. He is running out of time. He knows that we are on to him and that we are both too dangerous to live!'

Raising the telescope, he scanned the horizon, handed it to Faro. On the hillside, the tiny figures of the shooting party, so clear he could see their heads moving as they chatted, were making their way slowly down in the direction of Glasalt.

'We might as well do likewise,' said Purdie. 'Let me have another look. No. Absolutely no sign of Craig.'

'Where can he have got to?'

'He might have missed us, got lost and tagged on to the beaters. Yes, I imagine that's what has happened.'

As they walked downhill, Faro turned. Now far above them Noble had emerged from the boulder and was making a cautious descent with easel and painting materials.

The afternoon was still warm and the heather was filled with the steady drone of insects. Faro signalled a young beater to fetch Steady.

As Purdie yelled 'Drat them!' striking out ineffectually at the cloud of midges, Faro realised he had been too preoccupied with a different kind of attack to notice their very painful presence.

On the sloping lawn beside the Widow's House, where already the party had formed into groups, the picnic was being unpacked by the ghillies.

Brown solemnly withdrew a whisky bottle from the carriage. He held it high to the accompaniment of cries of delight.

'Just in case of need, ye ken,' he said straight-faced.

'Will it help my midge-bites, Brown?' called one of the ladies.

'Aye, if ye drink it down, it will help ye to forget them.'

Faro looked round the assembled throng. The Queen

was there with her pretty young daughter, Princess Beatrice, and their ladies-in-waiting; the two Captains Tweedie and Dumleigh, General Ponsonby, Mr Gladstone; the ghillies, Grant and Lachlan Brown; the beaters, young lads in rough tweeds, bonnets and shabby brogues.

Servants appeared from inside the house to dispense tea, scones and Dundee cake, all of which Faro thought fell far short of Aunt Bella's standards.

A party from Invercauld House made up the numbers. They were chiefly notable for their piercingly shrill English accents as Mr Gladstone regaled them with stories of his remarkable feats of hill-walking:

'. . . a mere bagatelle. Nineteen miles up Lochnagar. Came back fresh as a lark.' And patting his puffed-out chest, he surveyed them proudly. 'Sound as a bell. Not bad for a man past sixty, you'll agree.'

A burst of applause and delighted cries of 'Well done, Prime Minister,' brought a dour glance from the sovereign he tried so hard to impress.

Pausing in her conversation with Princess Beatrice she darted a glance, so frankly murderous, in Mr Gladstone's direction that Faro had to restrain himself from laughing out loud.

His eyes searched the little group. While their menfolk had indulged themselves with bringing down game birds on the hill, the ladies had prudently remained at Glasalt. Now they sat with their crinolines spread around them, a circle of pretty, gaily-coloured flowers on the grass, their faces protected from the insects' attacks by wide-brimmed hats and the dextrous use of fans.

The men, more soberly attired, lolled beside them, some daring Royal displeasure by lighting pipes and cigars. For once this activity failed to arouse the Queen's disapproval. Turning a blind eye on the wreaths of smoke ascending, she was prepared to be indulgent, persuaded by Brown that this kept the midges at bay.

Today she too abandoned formality to the extent of

sitting in a comfortable chair at a little distance and a little higher up the slope. She had chosen a position of vantage in keeping with her Royal image, from which she could look down approvingly upon the activities of her loyal subjects at play.

'It does make her look just a little like one of her many statues on a plinth,' murmured Purdie. And taking out a cigar, 'We might as well join the gentlemen. Care to?'

'Thank you, no.'

'Not even with a Royal dispensation?' Purdie smiled and then, noticing the two Captains, went on, 'If you will excuse me, Faro. I must have a word.'

A few moments later Faro observed him talking earnestly and found all three men staring fixedly in his direction.

Was Purdie telling them of his 'accident', warning them of the dangers now close at hand?

And scrutinising the faces in that merry carefree throng, were they what they seemed? Was this to be their only blood-letting, the massacre of game birds, their trophies spread out proudly before them on the grass?

And what troubled Faro most, where was Craig who up to now had been the shadow of the man from Scotland Yard? Why wasn't he here? Why hadn't he arrived to deliver Purdie's warning?

Who else was missing? He looked around. Noble. Where was he?

Somewhat unnerved still by his narrow escape, he would have enjoyed a pipe but decided instead to try out the cigars he had bought at the Crathie Inn. Taking Uncle Ben's silver case from the top pocket of his tweed jacket, he had just opened it when two footmen in liveried jackets but without wigs emerged from the house carrying drams on silver trays.

One was Peter Noble. As he approached Faro was about to ask him for a light when the footman whispered:

'If you would be so good, sir.'

And turning, Faro observed the ponderous face of the

Prime Minister staring fixedly in his direction, his imperious beckoning action indicating that Inspector Faro was to advance rapidly to where Her Majesty now engaged him in conversation.

Guiltily Faro snapped shut the cigar case, made his way up the slope and bowed to his sovereign. He had rather hoped his presence might not be noticed by the Queen on this occasion, for he was well aware that ahead now lay the interview he most dreaded.

He was right. The Prime Minister was dismissed with a chilly 'You may leave us.'

Mr Gladstone left dejectedly and the Queen gave Faro her full attention. 'And what have you to report to us? Have you been successful in your quest?'

'I am afraid not, ma'am. One can only conclude that Your Majesty's dogs were the victims of some person out shooting – rabbits,' he added lamely.

'We presume you have explored every avenue with your usual expertise, Inspector?'

'That is so, ma'am.'

'Then we are very disappointed, very. As you are aware, we are about to leave Balmoral. And we are not pleased that we must do so without the guilty man being apprehended and severely punished. Very severely indeed.' A thin smile, as she added, 'We have been led to understand that Inspector Faro is quite infallible. And indeed, so it has seemed. You have always been quite reliable in our service at Holyrood.' Her accompanying glance showed more of sorrow than of anger.

'Forgive me, ma'am, but the task was unusual and the animals—'

'Dash and Flash,' she provided sternly.

'Indeed, ma'am, as Dash and Flash had, er – passed on – some time before my arrival, I am afraid that whatever trail and clues might have existed, they had gone quite cold.'

Suddenly the Queen smiled, patted his hand. 'We

148

forgive you, Inspector. Brown has explained to us the diffi-
culties involved.'

'Thank you, ma'am.'

'After all, Brown has given us to understand that this
search for clues is quite a different matter to the work
usually undertaken by detectives.'

Faro, grateful to Brown for his intercession, bowed. He
refrained from adding that the Royal task was, in actual
fact, just one stage removed from rescuing old ladies'
cats stranded in the top branches of trees. A humble duty
that was most often the unhappy lot of the junior police
constable.

A shadow fell across the path. It was General
Ponsonby.

'Ma'am, it is now time for the salmon leistering to
begin.'

The Queen clapped her plump hands delightedly,
her giggle of pleasure transforming reigning monarch
momentarily into serving wench.

'We trust you will join us, Inspector.'

'I shall be honoured, ma'am.'

The assembled company rose, bowing as the Queen
went into the house followed by her ladies to attend to
their toilette.

As soon as they disappeared, an undignified scramble
ensued among the men. Drams had been lavishly re-
freshed throughout the picnic and although half of the
day's activity lay ahead, Faro could see that the whisky
flasks much in evidence during every shoot 'to keep the
cold out' had also been replenished. Now every half-
empty whisky bottle was seized upon.

Several of the party including one or two of the ladies
were in higher spirits than was reasonable for the time
of day, already in that condition the Queen was pleased
to describe as 'bashful'.

Faro guessed that once the sun sank behind the mountains and the leistering began not only the salmon would
be ready to succumb. As the men with bursting bladders

hastily sought relief in the little wood nearby, some had to be supported by their comrades.

Watching the exuberant groups emerge again, he wondered, was there hidden in their midst a murderer who behind a smiling mask coldly awaited his opportunity to kill the Queen?

And himself.

Chapter Twelve

The salmon leistering was traditionally an autumn activity
when the salmon were red and almost unfit for eating,
or so Faro remembered from reading Sir Walter Scott's
account in *Guy Mannering*.

At the Linn of Muick, a crowd had already gathered
to greet the Queen and her party in their conveyances.

Riding Steady alongside the fast-flowing river, Faro
saw that the floor of the glen was in deep gloom, the
sun dipping behind the tops of the mountains. The air
was suddenly chilly.

Cheers rose from the tenants drawn either by the
activity ahead or by the proximity of the Queen. They
lined the banks, the men bowing, removing bonnets, the
women curtseying as the Queen rode past, her daughter
at her side in her favourite open carriage, the 'sociable',
with Brown on the box.

When she had descended, a hand on his arm, he led
her to a vantage point from which she could have an
uninterrupted view of the proceedings.

The fishermen were already positioned awaiting the
signal.

The shout went up: 'Let the leistering begin.'

The word was passed along the river bank. The assembled tenants and fishermen waded into the water, poking
under the stones to dislodge lurking salmon, while others
waved torches back and forth to attract the fish to the
surface.

As they leaped, the men struck out with the leister,

a three-pronged implement reminiscent of Neptune's trident.

A flash of silver, a flash of iron and the salmon struggled once and was laid on the bank. Soon they were piled high, for those who escaped the tridents swam into a net.

Faro had positioned himself near the Queen. As the fever of the chase took over, he heard her deep laugh and once again remembered her taste for circus displays and wild animals.

In the gloaming, the weird long-lasting twilight of the Highlands, he dimly recognised Brown, Grant and Lachlan. Kilts tucked between their legs, they were walking the river, leisters upraised.

Perhaps encouraged by Her Majesty's cries, 'Oh, excellent. Well done,' some of the guests had joined them; rolling up trouser legs, they plunged laughing into the water. The sudden icy chill had its effect. Some were quickly sobered, while others, less steady, toppled from stones, took a drenching for their pains and came out shivering, much to their comrades' amusement.

Faro, seeing that Mr Gladstone and the two Captains had stationed themselves at the Queen's side, rushed down to lend a hand hauling out the inebriates.

And then tragedy threatened.

Further up water where the nets prevented the salmon leaping on to the higher reaches, the river became a rushing boulder-strewn tumult.

A small girl hovering on a rock, in her excitement, slipped and fell. Her screams were echoed by her mother. Hands were outstretched but, small and light, her clothes drenched, she was swept down towards the falls where she must be hideously broken and drowned.

Faro was never conscious of doing anything heroic. Acting instinctively, he threw off his jacket and leaped into the water.

As the child hurtled past him to the very edge of the falls, he managed to seize her skirts. A moment later, realising from her screams that she was terrified but otherwise unhurt, he handed her over to hands reaching out from the bank.

With danger over and everyone's attention diverted to the child now safely restored to her sobbing mother's arms, Faro was wading out of the shallows when something struck him hard in the small of his back.

The sudden pain shocked him, knocking the breath out of his body. He staggered backwards, backwards into the river where the raging waters, swiftly descending, seized him. His lungs full of water, blinded, he caught at an overhanging branch of a tree and clung on grimly. Shaking the water out of his eyes, he looked up, saw shocked faces above him.

The branch snapped and swirled towards the edge carrying him helpless with it. Faces mouthing words of warning lost in the deafening roar looked down at him.

Lachlan, Noble stretching out hands to him – but Purdie, older and stronger, was nearest. Faro held out his free hand desperately. Purdie had thrown himself face down, Faro grasped at his hand, missed, reached out again. This time he encountered two hands. Strong and firm, they held him.

Others followed and a moment later he was hauled on to the bank, panting, half-drowned.

Purdie bent over him. 'That was a near thing.'

'Too near, sir. You saved my life. Thank you.' Faro looked down at the boiling torrent. Another minute and if he hadn't drowned he would have been dashed to pieces on the rocks below.

'Think nothing of it,' said Purdie. 'But we had better get you home. I didn't save you from drowning to have you die of a fever.'

John Brown came running over with a blanket in Balmoral tartan. 'From the Queen, sir. Put it around you.'

Faro took it gratefully.

'Lachlan's away for your horse.'

As he waited whisky flasks were proffered, but he was already shaking like a man with an ague when Lachlan handed over the reins of Steady to him.

'Would you not rather have the carriage?' asked Purdie.

'No. No.'

'Are you sure?'

'I will be fine. I'm just cold. And one of us must stay with the Queen.'

By the time Steady had trotted briskly into Easter Balmoral and, unsaddled, was bedded down for the night, Faro was chilled to the bone.

But inside the cottage, the best sight in the world awaited him. Vince had called in only to find that Bella and Tibbie were out visiting neighbours.

Vince took one look at him, brought out the hip-bath, put it before the glowing peat fire, and while he boiled buckets and kettles of water, Faro gasped out the details of the child's rescue.

'And completely forgetting, of course, that you cannot swim.'

'It never occurred to me, lad. It didn't seem important.'

'You make me furious, sometimes,' said Vince angrily. 'Never did a man take less regard of his own skin. It's a mercy you weren't both drowned. Even a good swimmer would have been weighed down by the weight of those tweed trousers. And boots.'

He looked at the sodden heap, steaming by the fire.

'I'm afraid they'll never be the same again. But we hope you will.' Then he smiled, pouring another pan of boiling water into the hip-bath. 'A charmed life, that's what they say you have. I'm beginning to believe it.'

Half an hour later Faro, restored from his ordeal, was grimacing over a hot, strictly medicinal toddy as he related the events at Glen Muick. For Vince's benefit, he carefully omitted any sinister implications.

But Vince was not to be put off. 'How did you come by that very nasty bruise on your back?'

Vince had noticed it while he was sitting in the bath.

'When I fell down in the heather, I expect.'

'I thought you fell face forward?'

And when he didn't reply Vince continued with a look of triumph, 'Someone tried to kill you, Stepfather. Am I right?'

When Faro described what had happened, Vince said, 'Don't you think this has gone far enough? A daring rescue for a man who cannot swim is one hazard too many, when he has narrowly escaped death by walking in front of a shooting party.'

Vince shook his head. 'You are getting either very careless or remarkably absent-minded, neither of which are luxuries you can afford in your profession.'

It was scant consolation to realise that Inspector Purdie was not alone in failing to pick up obvious clues.

'Very well, but as you know, lad, I am the last to call "Wolf". There were a great many people milling about. Something hit me in the back, but it was over in an instant. I doubt if anyone noticed, all attention was on the wee lass. Besides, the gloaming can play tricks. Makes it damned difficult to see anything distinctly.'

'Sergeant Craig wasn't in the vicinity?'

'I didn't see him. I realise what you're thinking, but surely it cannot be Craig. After all, he is Purdie's right hand man. He must have had an arm's length of references to be trusted by the Yard.'

'And yet he did succumb to the money from Lachlan's bothy. Now that I would call irredeemable misconduct in a police officer. At the moment, Stepfather, I'd be prepared to lay even odds on Craig and Lachlan, as prime suspects.'

Faro, beginning to feel the effects of the day's travail, grew weary of the conversation, the cut and thrust of speculation. Normally relishing such discussion he now saw it as a great tide that led nowhere, sweeping him helplessly along unable to divert the disaster awaiting in the wings.

There was one direction he did not want it to lead. To Lachlan Brown.

'What do you think of Lachlan, by the way?' he asked trying to sound casual.

'Pleasant enough. Yes, very pleasant when he chooses to be so, I imagine.' Vince shrugged. 'I did not feel that we had a great deal in common. Except, of course, for fathers who had abandoned our mothers,' he added bitterly.

Faro suppressed a groan. Little did Vince know that the link of illegitimacy they shared was more intimate than he could ever have imagined. That there might exist an even stronger reason for Lachlan's resenting Vince, who had usurped his rightful position by becoming Jeremy Faro's son in every way but the accident of birth.

Faro closed his eyes before the awful prospect looming ahead of him. Vince's bitterness and hatred were unrelenting towards the unknown man who had fathered him. How would he react to the knowledge that his stepfather had similarly abandoned Inga St Ola and left her shamed in her Orkney home, forced to have their child fostered?

If the lad ever found out, whatever excuses he made, Vince would never really forgive him. Their whole future relationship could be blighted, put in jeopardy by a truth coming home to roost after more than twenty years.

Bella's clock melodiously struck nine, reminding him that he was to have had tea with Inga five hours ago – a momentous five hours in which he had twice escaped death.

He swore with some feeling.

'What's wrong, Stepfather?'

'I had an enagagement with a lady this afternoon. I forgot.'

'Inga?'

'The same. I had to go to Glen Muick instead, urgently. And it was too late to get a message to her.'

156

'Never mind, I suppose the Queen has precedence over all other ladies, including Inga St Ola.'

At Faro's faint smile, Vince said, 'How curious that she should come back into your life again. I mean, this connection with Lachlan Brown and so forth.'

'A strange coincidence indeed.'

'Do you know what I think, Stepfather?'

Although Faro knew perfectly well the pronouncement Vince was about to make, he shook his head obligingly.

'I think Inga and Lachlan are in this together.'

'Indeed. What evidence have you for that?'

'The evidence of my two eyes. You just have to look at them. Thick as thieves, they are.' He paused. 'I'm disappointed in you, Stepfather.'

'In what way?' Faro felt panic rising.

'Candidly, where are your powers of observation? They seem to be failing you badly of late.'

When Faro made no protest, Vince said, 'Obviously he wasn't born in Orkney or you would have heard all about him from Grandma. So it follows that the birth was kept secret. That some wretched man seduced her and left her. Just like my poor mother. But poor Inga did not have you—'

The wretched man in question wriggled uncomfortably, bit his lip. Listening to Vince's tirade, wanting to protest, No, it wasn't like that at all. He had not seduced Inga, although he was too much of a gentleman to say that it might well have been the other way round. Inga had loved him and his first experience of sex had not warned him of the consequences that might follow.

He wanted to protest that he never knew she was pregnant. If so, he would have married her.

Dammit, he had offered to do so.

'You knew her in those days, Stepfather.' Vince on the track of truth was relentless. 'You were a friend of hers, a cousin—'

'Much removed,' Faro interposed hastily.

'Could you not have advised her?'

157

'Vince, I was nineteen years old when I – when I knew her. She was twenty-one. Hardly the sort of thing she would seek to confide in me.'

'Did she never give any hint, I mean, about the man?'

'No,' said Faro shortly.

'Yet it must have been about the time you left for Edinburgh.'

Vince's earnest pursuit of right made him wince. 'Wait a minute, lad, here we are gossiping like a pair of old fishwives, tearing apart a lady's reputation when her story might be true.'

But Vince was not prepared to let go. 'You can't mean that Lachlan was fostered by her, really the son of a friend who died.' Pausing he gave a bark of laughter. 'Stepfather, you surely don't believe that. How can you be so simple? Why, that's the thinnest story I've ever heard.' And shaking his head sadly, 'I'm disappointed in you, really I am. Here you are, a master of deduction, unable to see through an obvious tissue of lies. Unless—'

'Unless what?' Faro demanded sharply.

Vince regarded him narrowly. 'Unless you don't want to solve this one,' he said softly.

And at that moment Faro suspected that in a flash of enlightenment Vince had solved the case for himself, the implication being that Lachlan was guilty of Morag's murder. Even as the monstrous thought took root, the scene at the river flashed vividly before him, touching a deeper, stranger chord of memory.

What was it? Something Vince had said earlier? But he was too tired to think and determined to be in bed before his aunt and Tibbie returned and subjected him to the inevitable ordeal of retelling the rescue story for their benefit, he bid Vince goodnight rather sharply.

He slept badly, nightmare scenes engulfing him. Over and over he was drowning with hands outstretched in front of him. But as he seized them, the fingers came

158

away like sticks in his hands and he hurtled backwards into the falls.

Next morning, hoping to escape with a light-hearted explanation for sodden garments left to dry by the fire, he found them all neatly pressed by Tibbie. As he related how he had slipped and fallen, how Inspector Purdie had rescued him, he remembered how strong his hands had been and the nightmare returned.

'You can overcome anything, if you will it.'

Anything but shrunken socks, it seemed, which he had placed on top of the hot oven.

But Bella, as always, had a solution close at hand.

From a drawer she took out a linen roll and withdrew a pair of kilt hose.

'This was the last pair I ever made for your uncle. Finished them the day he died and never had the heart to give them away. At my age, it's gey daft to hang on to things. It'll no' be long now afore we're t'gither again, an he'll say to me, "Bella, ye daft besom, ye always were a hoarder. Whatever came ower ye." So take them, Jeremy lad.' And burrowing further, 'This too, his skean dhu. Ye should have had it long since.'

Holding it, he remembered in an instant how his Uncle Ben had taught him to spin his bonnet on to the peg by the door. And by the same flick of the wrist, he had demonstrated how the skean dhu had been used in past ages with deadlier effect, to kill an enemy.

And Faro, saddling up Steady, was surprised to discover he had lost none of his expertise. He could still score a bull's-eye on the old beam above the door. But he expected less dazzling results with the excuses he had on hand to offer Inga St Ola.

On the way to her hotel he prepared himself for a very cool reception. Instead, Inga ran down the steps to meet him, grasped his hands.

Ready with his apologies he saw her expression was one of relief rather than anger.

'I am so sorry about yesterday—'

'It doesn't matter—'

'It is my own fault. I entirely forgot that I was to go out to Glen Muick—'

She shook her head. 'When you didn't arrive I realised that something had happened.'

Leading him to a garden seat, she sat down, spread her skirts and looked intently up into his face. 'I told myself that detectives are notoriously unreliable when they are engaged in the pursuit of criminals. And unexpected delays are the order of the day.'

At his startled expression, she continued, 'That's why you are here, is it not?'

Faro smiled wryly. 'I thought I was here for Aunt Bella's birthday and a fishing holiday. That, I assure you, was my intention.'

Inga laughed. 'Jeremy Faro, you'll be the death of me.'

'I'm glad you find me an object of mirth,' he said stiffly.

'I don't, I promise you.' And suddenly she was solemn. 'I don't. Anything but that. But I can guess that whatever you are supposed to be doing, the real reason is something very serious.'

A leaf fluttered down on to her lap and picking it up, she smoothed it out tenderly. 'I know you scorn this sort of thing, Jeremy, but I knew you wouldn't come.'

'Is that so? I assure you I do try to keep my word—'

'You don't understand. I don't mean it like that at all. Listen, I was looking forward to your visit. It was a lovely afternoon and then quite suddenly, it was all changed. Different. As if a giant shadow came across, between me and the sun.'

She looked around as if hoping to find some measure to fit the description. Then turning to him, she said, 'I knew you were in terrible danger. That your life at that moment hung by a thread. And there was nothing I could do – no warning I could give. So I concentrated hard, prayed, "Deliver him from evil."'

'What time was this, Inga?'

'Three o'clock had just struck on the hall clock.'

Faro looked away. He had checked his watch when he arrived in Glen Muick. Two thirty. He must have been walking for half an hour when he had fallen in the heather, the assassin's bullet cutting the air where a second before his head had been.

Mistaking his preoccupation, Inga sighed. 'I know it's silly and you disapprove, Jeremy. But I can't help it, I just know things. I don't want to but I do.' Smoothing out the leaf again, she shook her head miserably. 'I don't want to be a witch, but that's what I am.'

He took her hands, said softly, 'Your prayer worked, Inga. I nearly had a very nasty accident.'

'What happened?'

'Oh, I got in the way of the stalkers' guns—'

'Dear God, how awful—'

'My own stupid fault,' he said lightly, knowing he must not worry her further.

At that moment a bell sounded within the hotel. 'Would you care to stay for lunch with me?'

'I would love that.'

As they took their seats at a table overlooking the garden, he said, 'You were right. I am here on a case.'

'Can you talk about it?'

'I think so. It will make you smile to see how far is the mighty detective fallen.' He told her about the Queen's dogs and was grateful that she did not find it amusing. An animal lover, she considered it a serious matter, and worthy of his skill in detection.

'The Queen leaves tomorrow or the next day and I still haven't solved her mystery or produced her criminal.'

'Don't you think it was most likely an irate farmer?'

'I'm not sure. Perhaps you could use your second sight on that one?' And he laughed suddenly, placing his hand over hers on the table. 'What a team we would have made, Inga. Think of it. With your psychic powers and my practical ones. Quite unbeatable. Don't you agree?'

But his laughter died at the pain on her face. Contrite, he longed to say, Oh Inga, what did I – or Fate – between us do to you? All these wasted years, so empty and barren for you taking care of Saul Hoy whom you didn't love. And parted from Lachlan, whom you did.

He thought of the years they might have shared as husband and wife, and his mind raced ahead toying with the fleeting ghosts of other children they might have had. Instead he had Lizzie and Rose and Emily. And Vince, Lizzie's son – the lad dearer to him, he had told himself, than even his own son could have been.

As they were silent tackling the game soup which was steaming hot, he thought about the future.

After the Queen left Balmoral with danger and a national catastrophe averted, he would return to Edinburgh and to the less sensational everyday crimes that were the legacy of a great city. And in his own home, the pressing domestic problem posed by his housekeeper Mrs Brook and the care of her invalid sister.

As for the murder of Morag Brodie which had begun it all, that was Inspector Purdie's to solve. And he was thankful for once, that this was not his province.

He looked across at Inga. What on earth was he thinking about? Dear God, how could he go and leave her son, even if he wasn't his, to the mercy of the law? Especially if the lad was innocent. For he suspected a certain ruthlessness in the Inspector from Scotland Yard.

Purdie had a reputation to uphold and Faro guessed that he had already made up his mind that Lachlan, in the absence of any other suspect, must be guilty. In the Inspector's eyes, a suspect would be guilty until he was proved innocent.

There was no way to convince him unless, within the next thirty-six hours, Faro could produce the real criminal.

The maid interrupted his reverie, removing the soup plates and bringing in poached salmon. Inga smiled across at him.

'How long are you staying?'

'I shall be leaving on Saturday, in all probability. And you, Inga? What are your future plans?'

'I have applied for a situation of housekeeper. There are two possibilities in the area. Big houses, that sort of thing. And one with a professor in Aberdeen.'

'This is a big change for you.'

She shrugged. 'Without Saul, I have no desire to stay on Balfray. Besides, I want to be near Lachlan. It is all so different from the plan I made for this visit. I had thought to see him with a wife, a life of his own.'

'I thought you couldn't bear to leave Orkney.'

'Did I say that? It seems I did feel that way a long time ago. Now time seems to be running away from me, the old man with the scythe. The death of someone close always makes you aware that time is the enemy—'

He looked at her and thought how young she seemed; indestructible, this woman who was fast approaching middle age. Her black hair was still unstreaked with grey, eyes unlined, deep as bluebells, skin still satin-smooth.

'If Vince stays at the hospital, then who knows, we might all meet up again?'

With the turmoil she aroused in his heart, he wasn't sure that it was such a good idea.

As they prepared to leave, he apologised once again. 'I am sorry about yesterday. Truly.'

She shook her head, studying his face as if trying to remember every feature. 'It doesn't matter. As long as you are safe.'

Beyond the garden the distant river glittered silver. As he prepared to mount Steady, she watched him nervously, intently, smoothing on her gloves. Those gloves – another gesture he remembered.

His chaste goodbye kiss upon her cheek, she said, 'Be careful, Jeremy. That shadow, it's still over you, you know.'

The bright smooth lawn had been tranquil in sunlight. Suddenly the peace and stillness of that perfect autumn afternoon was invaded by a startled rookery, their raucous cries and ragged wings swirling overhead.

And he saw the sudden fear on her face as she glanced skywards.

Fear that neither would put into words.

Corbies. Those traditional birds of ill-omen.

Inga was watching them too. Closing her eyes, she was still as if for a moment she no longer occupied her body, still so shapely and comely, like that of a young girl.

'You're not out of the wood yet, Jeremy. There's danger, evil everywhere. All around you. And in the least expected places. Take care, dear friend, take care.'

Chapter Thirteen

Faro's route took him past the Crathie Inn to discover that Inspector Purdie had already left.

There was a message for him. He tore open the envelope.

'Plans are all changed. The Queen has announced her intention of remaining at Glasalt until her time of departure. I need not dwell upon the opportunities offered by a house so remote and virtually unguarded. *Come at once.*'

The last line was heavily underscored. Faro could imagine the chaos at the Castle, with frantic servants and only John Brown pleased since at Glasalt he enjoyed the full limelight of the Queen's informality.

In the light of his most recent deductions Faro had relived over and over in minute detail those desperate hours in Glen Muick. He had not the least doubt that Purdie was right.

The murder attempt would be made at the Widow's House.

The only hope of saving the Queen was in keeping one step ahead and in passing on certain vital information to Vince. But at Beagmill he was again thwarted. The two doctors had been called out to an accident case at a sawmill some ten miles distant.

Leaving an urgent message and praying that Vince returned in time, he set off for Ballater where he had some considerable difficulty in convincing Sergeant Whyte that he was in deadly earnest.

Following the bewildered policeman to the telegraph office, he stressed the urgency and hoped his two messages would be taken seriously by the startled clerk and not regarded as a hoax at their destinations.

Riding towards Glen Muick he decided that it was unlikely any attempt on the Queen's life would be made during the hours of daylight. At least such an attempt would not be made by one man acting alone, who would prefer to have the situation under his command with as few witnesses as possible.

In Glasalt he was interested to see the original numbers much depleted. Princess Beatrice and her lady-in-waiting had returned to Balmoral, for which he was grateful.

The young princess did not share her mother's enthusiasm for the great outdoors and on the excuse of a mildly sore throat had returned to the Castle. The excuse, flimsy as it might seem, was enough to alarm the Queen thoroughly, for her over-protection of 'Baby' included excessive worries about her health.

At the Queen's insistence, Mr Gladstone had also been returned to the Castle. He took a dour view of being deprived of the opportunity for another of his twenty mile walks through the hills.

A more willing member of the princess's escort was General Ponsonby, a worried man with much to arrange in the light of the Queen's changed plans. Captains Tweedledum and Tweedledee were firm in their resolve to remain. The Queen had somewhat ungraciously agreed.

To Brown in his rôle as temporary master of the household was given the task of allocating bedrooms. Built with an eye to accommodating guests, the main house contained several spare rooms and there were others in the so-called barn and stables outside.

In addition to the security guards, the party at Glasalt was now composed of the Queen, Lady Churchill, John Brown, and Inspectors Purdie and Faro. As for servants, Lachlan Brown would take care of the horses and Peter

Noble, a man of many accomplishments, would put aside his paint brushes and be in charge of supper.

Ponsonby left with a request for roast partridges, some salmon, chicken, Scotch trifle and Dundee cake: 'A simple picnic hamper plus two kitchen maids would be adequate.' The Queen had stressed also the need for lots of good wine.

She was less than delighted when they arrived under the personal supervision of her Prime Minister, who was determined not to let his sovereign out of his sight.

The Queen received his return with ill-concealed exasperation, almost rudely turning her back upon him as he bowed. Only Mr Gladstone was unaware of her petulant sigh of disapproval.

Faro had witnessed exchanges like this before and decided that Mr Gladstone was either deaf or insensitive, or conveniently, a little of both.

The Queen announced that all were here to indulge in pleasant relaxation and joyful activities. She would spend the afternoon sketching the view across the Loch of Darkness and Sorrow.

It now transpired that this was her urgent reason for remaining at Glasalt. The water-colour begun on her last visit was to be an anniversary present for Princess Vicky and her husband who were romantically inclined towards Deeside. For it was here that Prince Frederick had proposed. And while she painted, her lady-in-waiting, Lady Churchill, would read to her and Brown would remain in attendance.

Accordingly the visitors dispersed. The Captains elected for fishing, and Faro's sharp eyes detected a couple of rifles, hard to conceal, as unlikely fishing rods among their equipment.

'Have you any plans, Faro?' Purdie asked.

Faro decided to keep these to himself. He spoke vaguely of riding along the shore of the loch.

'You wouldn't care to accompany me?' Purdie enquired.

'I thought I might go in search of our missing policeman. A good walk would do us both good.'

Unfortunately this was overheard by Mr Gladstone and nothing short of a deliberate insult could dissuade him from accompanying the Inspector, who gave Faro a despairing gesture.

Noble left the house with them, carrying his easel, determined to complete his painting of Glasalt unless light and weather failed him.

Faro had his own reasons for a careful search of the hill where his life had been threatened. Brown's two collie dogs watched wistful-eyed the guests assembled in the yard. He was calling them to heel when Faro asked:

'Would they come with me?'

'Aye. They would that.'

'Very well. Come!'

'Are you sure you wouldn't care to join us, Faro?' said Purdie, viewing dogs and horse with curiosity.

Gladstone, whose speech on the splendid qualities of hill-walking and his own indomitable prowess was in full flood, viewed this interruption with disfavour. Faro watched the two men depart with some amusement, even the younger, taller Inspector having problems matching his stride to the elder man. At last Gladstone's voice faded and the two disappeared.

Faro rode up the hill and stopped to take out the field glasses which were always accessible at Glasalt. Noble was approaching the boulder where they had met the previous day, while Tweedie and Dumleigh were heading downwards to the loch.

Faro took stock of his surroundings. He was going to need a great deal of luck to find what he sought on that wild desolate hillside where Craig had disappeared so mysteriously.

He found that stalking was in fact a great deal easier in the heather than in the streets and wynds of Edinburgh, especially with a couple of borrowed dogs.

His search was rewarded, alas, and it was a sadder if

considerably more enlightened Faro who started back for Glasalt. The fact that his theory about the second shot had proved correct did nothing to alleviate his distress as a chill mist rose from the loch and embraced him.

There were few things which struck naked terror into his heart, but fog – heavy blanketing fog, silent and unrelenting – was one of them. For years he had been unable to find one good sound reason to account for such a nonsensical fear in a grown man.

In Edinburgh, when Arthur's Seat disappeared from his window for several days at a time, when the top storeys of the tall High Street 'lands' vanished into swirling mist and day folded imperceptibly into night, he was consumed by supernatural fears. As the streets filled with the ghostly echoes of horses and riders looming out of nowhere to be immediately lost again, he was gripped by a primeval horror of the unknown which defied all his powers of rationalisation.

It was Vince who found the solitary clue to his stepfather's strange phobia which he would have been ashamed to admit to any of his colleagues. Vince believed that it belonged to the time when his father, Constable Magnus Faro, was run down by a carriage in heavy fog on the High Street. Faro was four years old.

An understanding of the origins of his fear did nothing to comfort him in his now certain knowledge of what lay in wait at Glasalt Sheil. He realised the importance of keeping his discovery to himself. His only hope of outwitting his adversary was to play for time and pray that his messages had been believed.

The Queen's life was at stake and there were few at hand to defend her. Should any premature move or alarm be made, he had no doubt that the assassin would strike fast and a bloody end ensue.

Despite his urgency, the man whose inbuilt sense of direction was a legend in the Edinburgh City Police failed dismally in the face of rapidly descending fog. He proceeded to get himself well and truly lost. Taking the wrong track, twice he landed up on what he thought were the shores of Glen Muick only to find that between himself and the path to Glasalt were sixty yards of bog-marsh.

Steady, it seemed, shared his unease. The dogs meanwhile had disappeared. He whistled in vain; presumably they were near enough home to have deserted him for the warmth of the stables, while the other guests at the first signs of the descending mist had wisely reassembled at Glasalt.

An hour later Faro's non-arrival was the signal for alarm. The Prime Minister was organising a search party when horse and rider appeared through the gloomy murk of the stable yard.

Gladstone seemed a little put out by Faro's return. He had rather liked the idea of being on the trail of a detective inspector, whose methods of detection he would claim he found difficult to assess. The policeman had been unable even to find the simple solution to who had killed the Queen's dogs.

Although Glasalt supposedly signified informal living, some of the proprieties were to be observed. Accordingly they all stood by their chairs round the table in the little sitting-room, until a bell rang and the Queen appeared.

Faro wondered if half an hour would be the statutory allowance for this so-called leisurely meal, as he understood was the rule in Balmoral.

That soon appeared to be the case. All was silent but for the clash of cutlery, the pouring of wine, and the scraping of plates. The other diners refused all his attempts to engage in polite conversation. They had been here before, he soon realised from their warning glances in the direction of the Queen who gobbled her food at an alarming rate.

The Royal Scotch broth plate was emptied, bread demolished before it seemed the other diners had taken more than two spoonfuls.

At Faro's side, Captain Dumleigh belched quietly and

170

refused the fish course. 'My indigestion,' he whispered. 'It is hell. Now you understand why.'

'I wanted to tell you—'

'Don't waste time,' said Captain Tweedie, timing his actions to coincide with the Queen's next course. 'I beg of you. Just keep eating, or you'll be starving by morning.'

Faro managed only half his salmon before the plate was whipped away. Resentfully he glanced towards the Queen who was drumming her fingers on the tablecloth, impatiently awaiting the next course.

With warning, he did better by the chicken and by refusing the Scotch trifle, kept well abreast of the field of diners. Realising, however, that his stomach was never his strong point, he knew he would be exceedingly fortunate not to end the day with a severe bout of indigestion.

If he was still alive.

Half-past eight struck. The Queen rose and went over to the piano. Accompanying herself she sang a Schubert *Lied* in German. The words meant nothing to Faro, but he could tell by her expression that it was a sad, sad song.

She was loudly applauded and smiling, wiped away a tear.

'Most affecting,' whispered Gladstone. 'One of Prince Albert's favourites. They used to sing it together.'

With the mist swirling at windows already streaked with fine rain, a cheerful fire proportionally larger than those which warmed Balmoral Castle did little to dispel Faro's fears.

The Queen was waxing poetic about Scotland, saying how sorry she was to leave Balmoral and claiming this was because of her descent from the ill-fated Queen Mary. Touching Brown's arm, she whispered. He nodded and went out to return with Lachlan.

The Queen smiled. Indicating the piano she said:

'Come, Lachlan, you shall be our Rizzio.'

Faro felt his throat constrict. This was indeed a most unfortunate simile, he thought, remembering that other

171

ill-fated supper room in Holyrood where more than three hundred years ago a Queen had been entertained by her secretary who had died minutes later clinging to her skirts with thirty-seven stab wounds in his body. That supper room still retained for Faro something of that terrible atmosphere as if the scene had frozen into the walls. For Rizzio's death had set the pattern for a series of catastrophes from which, those with Jacobite inclinations would claim, Scotland had never recovered.

A moment later, listening to Lachlan's playing, Faro realised that the lad was a gifted performer. A music lover himself, his favourite activity was going to concerts at Edinburgh's Assembly Hall. He had heard the finest in the realm and recognised with awe that he was in the presence of a born musician.

The Queen however seemed quite indifferent. She chattered to Lady Churchill and prevailed upon her to play dummy whist. Lachlan's playing of a Mendelssohn concerto failed to interrupt the slap of cards on the table and the Queen's joyous triumph over her lady-in-waiting.

Meanwhile the rain on the window intensified. Where was Vince? Why hadn't help arrived? Faro, feeling trapped, was conscious of the enormity of what was about to happen.

Purdie obviously was also uneasy. Lachlan ceased playing and to applause conducted by Faro, bowed and left the room.

Purdie, catching Faro's eye, led him to a far corner of the room and whispered, 'We must talk. We must make some sort of plan. I have told Brown of our fears. He found them amusing. Amusing! Can you credit that? I told him we intend to remain in the house tonight and if necessary we will sleep outside the Queen's bedroom door.'

Producing a roughly drawn plan of the house, he said, 'Any attack will be made during the hours of the night. Here is the Queen's bedroom and next door

Lady Churchill's. On the floor above, John Brown. The Captains have been allocated rooms next door to her. Servants in the stables—'

Purdie paused, held up his hand. 'Listen. Did you hear that?'

Faro looked towards the fire with its crackling logs.

'No.' Purdie interpreted his gaze. 'A shot. From outside.'

Springing to his feet, bowing briefly towards the Queen who was oblivious to everything but the fact that she held a hand with several trump cards, he said to Faro, 'You stay here.'

'I'm coming with you.' Faro was about to follow him when his way was blocked by Mr Gladstone who wanted a full account of how a detective inspector had managed to lose himself on the hill that afternoon.

Trying to withdraw with speed and tact was an impossibility. A minute later, no longer caring for politeness, he shouted, 'You must excuse me, Prime Minister,' and bolted.

Purdie had disappeared. Faro called several times, his voice swallowed by the thick mist. The only sounds were of the trees dripping mournfully, while somewhere close at hand a sheep lamented.

Closing the front door behind him, he walked round the house carefully, but there was no sign of a lurking intruder or of Purdie. Entering by way of the kitchen door he found Captain Tweedie vigorously stirring powder into a glass.

'Bicarbonate of soda. Dumleigh is suffering agonies of indigestion. We've made our excuses to Her Majesty.' And suppressing a yawn he added, 'If we are to be fit for this night vigil, we had better get Dumleigh on his feet again.'

'Is there anything I can do?'

'Not a thing. All Dumleigh needs is to lie low and let this take effect. Noble is bringing us a hot toddy, just to make sure.'

Faro went up to the room he was to share with Purdie but as he had expected it was ominously empty. He was overcome by a sudden feeling of helplessness and despair that the situation was running away from him, that in this case he was no longer in control and too much had already been lost.

Taking from his valise the gun he had acquired in Ballater and his uncle's skean dhu for good measure, he ran downstairs. The corridor leading to the sitting-room was dimly lit and intensely cold, the domestic scene heart-warmingly normal as Faro opened the door.

The party had broken up with the departure of the two Captains. Mr Gladstone, lacking an audience, greeted his arrival with delight.

Of Brown there was no sign. And where was Purdie?

The Royal game of dummy whist continued with the slap of cards on the table. The Queen, either by luck or design, was winning as usual.

'My trick, I think,' she said. 'And another – and another. For goodness' sake, my dear, why did you not play your trumps?'

Lady Churchill wisely pretended not to hear.

This time there was no escape from Mr Gladstone who put down his *Lives of the Saints* with some eagerness. Advancing upon Faro, he picked up the threads of their broken conversation as if in fact Faro had not retreated in mid-sentence.

The clock struck nine. It had been a long evening which would soon end with the welcome sight of hot toddies all round. 'To keep out the cold', as Brown put it.

As the minutes ticked by, the ponderous question and answer game with the Prime Minister had been transformed into a monologue on the benefits of hill-walking to one's health and moral fibre.

Faro's mild protest about the weather brought forth the stern rejoinder, 'God made the elements, sir. They all have their place in His universe. It is not our place to question His will.'

The Prime Minister now switched from the perfection of healthy exercise to the imperfections of the criminal mind. Despairingly, Faro hardly heard Mr Gladstone's theories, his mind on Purdie's disappearance. Suddenly he realised that the Prime Minister nursed secret longings to be a detective.

His discourse was momentarily interrupted as the footman slid a tray of hot toddies on to the sideboard just inside the door.

The Queen's frugality in the matter of candles was firmly adhered to in the Widow's House, where all the illumination was centred on the fireside and an oil lamp provided for card players.

With his back to them, Noble added glasses to the jug on the tray. His livery now included his white wig, although such spruceness could hardly matter in this informal atmosphere, thought Faro, as he was not required to serve them individually.

As the door closed behind the footman, Mr Gladstone frowned at this new diversion. 'It appears that we are to help ourselves.'

Faro sprang to his feet. 'Allow me, sir.'

'Not Her Majesty,' warned Gladstone. 'She, er, makes her own arrangements with Brown.'

At Faro's questioning look, he added, 'It is traditional. They share a last dram together, after everyone else has retired. Including Lady Churchill. Her Majesty dismisses her last of all. The poor lady sleeps badly and is allowed to take a sleeping draught,' he said with a disapproving shake of the head.

At the door Faro noticed that Noble's spruce appearance had not extended to wiping his boots which had carried a great deal of mud into the room.

He offered the tray to Lady Churchill who declined sharply. 'I never do, thank you.'

The Queen, intent on her game, slapped down another fan of cards. 'Our game, I think. We have won again,' she cried delightedly.

175

As Faro hovered indecisively, Lady Churchill whispered, 'Brown serves Her Majesty.'

Prim but eager, Mr Gladstone took the glass, stared at the contents and with an apologetic 'Just to keep the cold out. I am a poor sleeper you know,' drank the contents at one gulp.

Faro took one sip and hurriedly replaced the glass on the tray. He was a purist where whisky was concerned and disliked the addition of sugar and hot water. That for him savoured too much of Vince's 'medicinal purposes', his constant remedy for his stepfather's upset stomach.

As he returned the tray to the sideboard, the door opened to admit Brown who took it from him. 'Let me do that, Inspector.'

And noticing the muddy footprints, Brown shook his head and whispered, 'I'll need to get one of the servants on to that. The Queen's a stickler for clean floors. Have you no' had your toddy, Inspector?'

'I prefer mine undiluted.'

'Aye, that's the way of it for me too. But we have to humour the Queen,' he added pouring some of the jug's contents into a glass. 'Shame to desecrate good usquebaugh, the water of life.'

And taking a large sip, he paused to grimace. 'This is awfa' stuff, right enough. Too spiced, half cold. I have my own secret receipt for the Queen's toddy.'

Faro glanced sideways at the Prime Minister who seemed to have subsided into his chair. Brown's entrance had mercifully doused his monologue on the peculiarities of the Scottish law verdict 'Not Proven'.

Perhaps, Faro decided uncharitably, disliking the Queen's faithful servant, he had relinquished any part of a conversation which did not allow him the full share of the limelight.

With a glance over his shoulder towards the card players, Brown said: 'Ken how I got Her Majesty to take tea? Never cared for it as a lass and made outdoors with tepid water, even with the Prince's patent stove which never worked . . . ' His shudder was expressive. 'One day, ye ken, she asked what blend it was and so forth, said it was the best cup o' tea she had ever tasted. Do ye ken what I tellt her?'

Faro shook his head. 'Well, I said to her, So it should be, ma'am. I put a grand nip o' whisky in it,' Brown added, slapping his thigh.

As Brown was refilling his glass, Faro noticed that he was not quite steady on his feet. The reason for his absence now obvious, wondering how long he had been imbibing, Faro narrowly averted disaster to a small table bearing a collection of priceless Meissen china.

The Queen, alerted, said sharply, 'Brown, isn't it rather early in the evening for that?' and returned to her game.

Brown bowed, apologised and sat down in the chair rather heavily. He yawned. 'Dinna ken what's come over me, Inspector.' And yawning deeply again, 'I'm that sleepy, all of a sudden.'

As Brown's head dropped on to his chest, Faro turned his attention to Mr Gladstone, now slumped back into his chair and breathing heavily.

He was fast asleep. And snoring loud enough to alert the Queen. He would never forgive himself. He would be convulsed with embarrassment if his behaviour was noticed.

Faro leaned forward. 'Prime Minister, you were saying?'

There was no movement.

The Queen turned, frowning.

'The Prime Minister seems to have dropped off, ma'am'.

'So we hear, Inspector. So we hear.'

'Shall I waken him?'

A Royal gesture of dismissal. 'By no means, Inspector. All this healthy air, all these interminable walks have taken their toll. Let sleeping ministers be.'

Her eyes slid over Brown in the chair opposite. 'The drink makes him bashful.'

'He will sleep it off, ma'am,' said Lady Churchill wearily. 'He usually does.'

The Queen smiled at Faro. 'Silence is such a relief, do you not agree?'

And mercifully not awaiting an answer, she turned back to dealing the cards while Faro contemplated the sleeping Prime Minister with an ominous sense of dread.

He took up the glass again, sniffed it. Another tentative sip told him the truth. The hot toddies were drugged.

He walked to the window, stared through the curtains. The small astragals made it safe against breakage or intruders.

The card players were also out of range. Bowing himself out of the room, he glanced into the empty kitchen on his way upstairs to alert the two Captains.

There was no answer to his tapping on the door. Thankfully finding it unlocked he went inside. A candle burned between the two beds. Sprawled on one was the inert shape of Captain Dumleigh; on the other lay Tweedie.

Dumleigh was more heavily asleep than could be accounted for by the empty glass of bicarbonate of soda. The toddy glass on the bedside table accounted for the other Captain.

Faro ran downstairs. Where was Noble? And most of all what had happened to Inspector Purdie?

As he stood indecisively in the kitchen, he realised that the two maids must have retired, leaving a scene of disorder.

Lachlan Brown too. Where was he?

At that moment he heard a scuffling from one of the large pantry cupboards.

Mice? Rats?

A faint voice, female, from inside. 'Help – please help.'

The door was locked.

'All right. All right. I'll get you out.' Faro looked round for the key. There was one on the windowsill. Would it fit?

As it turned in the lock and he threw open the door, the two maids who had been inexpertly tied up and gagged, stared sobbing up at him.

He unfastened the ropes that bound them, and removed the elder maid's gag first. She gasped, 'Oh, sir. The Lord be thanked. We thought you might be him again.'

'Him? Who did this to you?'

'Lessing. It was Lessing, sir.'

'Lessing – the footman?'

'Yes, sir.' The two were gibbering with fear.

'It was his ghost, sir. He came into the kitchen—'

'Back from the dead,' shrieked the other servant. Her voice rising to a horror-stricken scream, she pointed over Faro's shoulder.

'There – there.'

Faro turned to see the bewigged footman standing in the doorway.

'It's me you want, Faro. I'm waiting for you. I've been waiting a long time.'

The face was half-hidden but he recognised the voice.

The two servants screamed again, but Faro had no time to attend to them.

'That's no ghost. And he intends to kill the Queen.'

With no further explanation, Faro plunged out into the mist after Lessing. Other footsteps passed nearby and he seized the man who was rushing towards him.

It was Lachlan Brown.

Chapter Fourteen

'I think I've just seen a ghost,' Lachlan panted. 'Lessing, the footman. Came at me like a bat out of hell. I thought he was dead—'

'He is very much alive, alas. Have you a gun?'

'Yes, but not here.'

'Take this, then.' As Faro handed him the gun, he looked at it doubtfully. 'Can you use one of these?'

'I think so.'

'For God's sake, lad, don't just think. The Queen is in deadly danger and I'm going after Lessing.'

'Where's Johnnie?'

'He's been drugged.'

'Drugged – Johnnie?'

'And the Captains and Mr Gladstone. In the hot toddies.' And cutting short Lachlan's bewildered questions, 'Where's Noble?'

'He took your horse. Said he had an errand. I thought you had sent him—'

Taking Lachlan by the arm Faro ran towards the sitting-room. Opening it cautiously, he was relieved to hear the Queen's voice and Lady Churchill's. Heavy breathing continued to emanate from the slumped figures of Brown and the Prime Minister.

As he had expected there was no key in the lock.

Lachlan watched him as if he had taken leave of his senses.

'Listen. You're to stand guard here. Outside the sitting-room. And do not leave your post. Whatever happens. Do you understand?'

'I wish I did—'

'The Queen is in deadly danger. If Lessing tries to get into that room: Shoot him.'

As he rushed outside, the fog enveloped Faro like a shroud. An unhappy simile, he thought shuddering. Perhaps that was the reason he had hated and feared the fog, that somewhere out there lay his death.

Angry with himself he switched from fear to practicality. How could he find anyone in this murk? He could not stray from the house but it was imperative that he should intercept Lessing, disarm him before he could get back inside. If he failed then only Lachlan stood between the Queen and murder.

He realised with growing horror that he was not ready for this, had never been ready for it. The momentum of events had taken him by surprise. Lessing's plan was brilliantly calculated to seize full advantage of the weather and the Queen's unexpected isolation.

He should have taken into account the cunning of his adversary. He should have stayed one step ahead but even visibility now ended at the garden wall and with it all hopes of taking the murderer by surprise.

From out of the mist every faint sound alerted him that the positions were reversed. Hunter into hunted, pursuer into pursued.

Lessing. The letters jumbled together in his head. Lord Nob's aliases were all anagrams of 'Noblesse oblige', the enigmatic clues to his real identity.

For once Faro had been blinded by his own deduction. By taking coincidence as fact, he had committed the worst transgression of a detective. He had under-estimated the power of his adversary.

He was still considering his next move when he heard Purdie's voice.

'Faro. Faro, I'm over here. Where the devil are you?'

Turning, Faro saw through the gloom the kitchen door open and close. As he raced towards it, expecting to find it bolted against him, it flew open and the muffled cries from inside the pantry indicated that the maids had been locked up again.

His back towards him, Lessing was bending over a huddled form on the floor. Lachlan Brown.

'Did you need to do that?'

Lessing turned round. Without the wig and livery jacket, Faro still had difficulty in recognising him as his old adversary from the Case of the Killing Cousins. A man with a hundred faces, the chameleon features of the born actor.

But when he spoke it was in Purdie's voice.

'So we meet again. Hand over your gun, if you please.'

And waving a gun towards the still figure of Lachlan Brown, he urged, 'Come along, Faro. If you tarry, I'll be forced to put a bullet through his head.'

'I am unarmed. I gave him my gun.'

'So that's where it came from. I'm much obliged to you. I need your help—'

'You'll get no help from me—'

Lessing ignored the outburst. 'But you are the key figure in my drama,' he said reproachfully.

Ignoring that, Faro asked, 'Who is buried in Lessing's grave?'

'Sit down. Do as I say. That's better. How should I know who they buried? Drowning fitted my plan excellently. Craig had already been recruited by our friends and sent here to await "Inspector Purdie's" arrival. A gossip in the local inn was all he needed to find out Purdie's childhood associations with the area, while he kept a sharp lookout for a likely candidate to double as Lessing's poor drowned corpse. The tinkers' arrival for the Ghillies' Ball would doubtless provide a conveniently drunken vagrant roughly my height and size. Unless we were very unfortunate.'

He shrugged. 'The rest was easy. Our last encounter on a clifftop in Orkney has, I am sure, convinced you that I am a swimmer of considerable ability, with a talent for survival. Indeed, I was once awarded a medal for life-saving.'

182

His laugh was without humour. 'Life-saving, Faro. Is that not capital, considering your present circumstance? But I digress. Craig had dry clothes ready and a corpse awaiting my swim downstream. When Morag saw her ring on his finger, she was certain to reel from closer examination of features battered beyond recognition. Meanwhile Craig kept me conveniently hidden in an empty cottage until it was time for Morag to leave us.'

'Did you have to kill the girl too?'

'I am afraid so. She was becoming burdensome. I did not much like being followed or the prospect of being father to her child. The idea of luring her to the mill and transporting her body on to Brown's doorstep, as it were, appealed to me.

'Surely you get the picture, Faro. That it was absolutely essential for someone at Balmoral to be murdered so there would be a police investigation requiring the skills of the bogus Inspector. We had to have a murder suspect and we both know how eagerly the local police would seize upon Lachlan Brown. Especially when that ridiculous custom of Scots marriage and the anonymous and highly suspicious annuity, which we had so generously arranged, became known. The Prince's Party leave nothing to chance and their forged papers are a credit to them. We even killed the Queen's spaniels in case they raised the alarm about the bogus footman.'

'Who *are* these people?' Faro interrupted.

'That, I am not at liberty to disclose. Not even to you, Faro, as your dying wish—'

'Is the Prince involved?'

'Bless your innocence, Faro. Can you see the future King of England condoning regicide – not to mention matricide. After all, this is the nineteenth century, we are supposed to be civilised.'

Again the laugh that accompanied his statement chilled Faro's blood.

'As far as His Royal Highness knows, we are a bunch

of harmless fanatics, worshipping at the shrine of his popularity.'

'And the real Inspector Purdie?' asked Faro, eager to keep him talking, aware that his one forlorn hope lay in playing for time. And that Lord Nob's vanity and pride in his own cunning were his only weaknesses. He could never resist telling his victims how he had outwitted them.

Before he killed them.

'Our information from a source at Scotland Yard was that the Inspector was to be on a fishing holiday in the north of Scotland. Beard and spectacles were always a problem. I realised that this was a rôle I could not sustain indefinitely or indeed for more than a few days. And that if you saw me as Lessing, as I appeared to Nessie Brodie as her last visitor, then the game would be up. But see how beautifully it has all fallen into shape. Even Her Majesty has obliged us by her change of plans. I can tell you, it was going to be deuced difficult at Balmoral. But this, my dear Faro, is a walkover. Almost too easy.'

'What about Craig?'

'He had to be disposed of, alas.'

'I know. I found him.'

'You did? When?' A faint shadow crossed Lessing's face.

'This afternoon. The dogs nosed him out in a crevasse on the hill. Where you had shot him. I'd like to know why?'

'He failed to fulfil his early promise and there is no room for mistakes in our organisation. He was supposed to kill you on the hill, make it look like an accident. Instead he fell victim to the second shot. Craig had no finesse. Very useful for stealing things like drugs from the hospital while I kept the good doctors occupied. But behaving like the small-time criminal, stealing money from the main suspect – such behaviour threw our whole operation into hazard.'

184

He paused, smiling. 'As did your survival of the shooting accident. I decided on a brilliant new rôle for you, one I had in mind for John Brown originally. For when the Queen is found dead, you will have shot her. And then, alas, taken your own life. Is that not a neat twist? And such a scandal. A pity you won't be able to read about it in all the newspapers.'

'What have you done with Noble?'

Lessing smiled. 'When I rushed out to destroy all evidence of Purdie, I told him the Queen was in danger. He was to go to Ballater for help. He obligingly threw off his wig and livery jacket which were essential for me to play the footman. Poor Noble hates horses. I shouldn't be surprised if he doesn't come to an unhappy end in this weather—'

A clock struck the hour. Lessing looked round uneasily.

'How did—' Faro began.

'No more questions, Faro. I have no more time to give you. Much as I always enjoy pitting my wits against yours, this will be our last meeting. I must confess I'm disappointed in you, Faro. You haven't been very clever this time and now you have to pay the price of bunglers.'

Even as Lessing pointed the gun, Faro had one final chance. Seizing the skean dhu from his sock, he hurled it.

Lessing staggered, fell. But Faro saw, too late, that the knife had struck his shoulder. He was only superficially wounded. As Faro leaped towards him, Lessing raised the gun, fired once.

The whole world exploded in pain. And as Faro slid slowly to the floor, he saw his own blood oozing from his chest.

So it was all over. All that remained now of the long career of Detective Inspector Jeremy Faro, was the trivial business of dying.

Far away he seemed to hear the drum of hoofbeats,

voices, and a door opening. The Queen's voice raised in a shrill scream.

As his eyes closed he had one last wish: that he had been able to discover if Lachlan Brown was truly his own son.

It was one mystery he would never solve, an answer thrown to the winds of time.

For a long while the darkness enveloped him, but when he once more opened his eyes, it was to a small white world bounded by sheets, pillowcases, white walls.

He was in hospital in Beagmill, with Vince bending over him.

'That was a near thing, Stepfather. We thought we were too late—'

'The Queen?' Faro whispered.

'She's in London. Safe and sound.'

'Lessing?'

'Awaiting trial.'

The leaves outside the window were golden.

'How long have I been here?'

'A week.' Vince held up a cigar case, with a neat bullet hole plugged into it. 'If it hadn't been for this, nothing, no one could have saved you.'

And little by little, Vince pieced the story together for him. His messages had reached Aberdeen City Police who had quickly telegraphed Scotland Yard to find the real Inspector Purdie returned from holiday due to a family bereavement. The police had immediately summoned the Gordon Highlanders regiment from the Bridge of Don barracks and it was a small army, hampered by the swirling mist, that Noble met riding towards Glen Muick with Dr Elgin and Vince in their midst.

'We had just returned to the hospital. There'd been a bad accident at a sawmill. We had to do some amputations on the spot. And then that damned mist. Then we got your message.

'I shall never forget the scene at Glasalt, Stepfather.

186

Never. Like the last act of *Hamlet* with a touch of the Sleeping Beauty's Palace. Lessing was taken prisoner. He's awaiting trial. It will be a sensation—'

'Lachlan Brown?'

'Nothing but a dunt on his head. Seems he put up a good fight though. He's gone to London with John Brown. Using Saul Hoy's legacy to study music.'

Faro nodded. He was unlikely to meet the lad again. It was just as well. But the boy's mother hadn't quite finished with him.

Vince was telling him, 'Inga has been in regularly each day to see you and so have Great-aunt and Tibbie. All the flowers are theirs.'

'I expect Aunt Bella was very upset about Uncle Ben's cigar case?'

'On the contrary, she's delighted. You can imagine the story she's making of that. And his skean dhu. How Uncle Ben reached out from the grave to save his favourite nephew.'

'Why is Inga still here?'

'She wanted to see you well again. And she's still hoping for a housekeeper's situation. She'll be back later this evening.'

Vince paused reflectively. 'I was just thinking. The problem with our Mrs Brook and her ailing sister. We could solve it by having Inga as our housekeeper—'

'We could, lad. But I think we won't.'

Vince looked at him intently. 'Then I will refrain from asking why not, Stepfather. Because if I tried very hard I might rightly guess your private reasons for such a decision.'

Faro was grateful for the sudden change of subject when Vince said, 'Tell me, how did you get on to Lessing being Purdie?'

'I almost didn't. Until too late. I should have seen it earlier. Purdie who had grandparents in the area and had stayed here as a child but was ignorant about the skean dhu and Scots marriage customs. But I was blinded by

187

working with a distinguished Scotland Yard detective and by the damnable coincidence that the name 'Noble' fitted 'Noblesse oblige' to perfection.

'It was Aunt Bella's story of the real Purdie's missing fingers that gave me the clue. A boy who loses fingers in childhood from his right hand will almost certainly begin to use his left. But Lessing was instinctively right-handed.

'But it wasn't until after he rescued me from the water that night that I realised that, without his gloves, he had two whole, strong hands. It must have irked him not to let me go, but in front of so many witnesses . . . '

'I imagine he saw that making you feel beholden to him was a marvellous move,' said Vince. 'How could you then ever suspect the truth?'

In the post came a letter from Buckingham Palace. It was from the Queen herself commending Inspector Faro's bravery.

'It appears I am to be presented with a medal,' he told Vince and putting aside the letter, he began to laugh, choking, helpless.

'What is it, Stepfather?' Vince demanded in alarm.

Faro was remembering the last thing he had heard before he lost consciousness in Glasalt.

Brown, with a stronger head than most, had been groggily awakened by the sound of a shot. The Queen, her card-playing disturbed by the ensuing uproar, had stamped out into the corridor, observed her favourite ghillie swaying into the kitchen and was shrilly demanding:

'Brown, are you bashful again?'